OF TIME AND STARS

The Worlds of

ARTHUR C. CLARKE

LONDON

VICTOR GOLLANCZ LTD

1983

First published August 1972
This edition March 1983

British Library Cataloguing in Publication Data
Clarke, Arthur C.
  Of time and stars.
  I. Title
  823'.914[J]   PZ7

  ISBN 0-575-03315-0

Printed in Great Britain by
St Edmundsbury Press, Bury St Edmunds, Suffolk

Contents

	Page
Foreword	7
The Nine Billion Names of God	11
An Ape About the House	20
Green Fingers	29
Trouble with the Natives	36
Into the Comet	52
No Morning After	65
"If I Forget Thee, Oh Earth . . ."	73
Who's There?	79
All the Time in the World	86
Hide and Seek	101
Robin Hood, F.R.S.	115
The Fires Within	121
The Forgotten Enemy	132
The Reluctant Orchid	141
Encounter at Dawn	153
Security Check	168
Feathered Friend	174
The Sentinel	179
Bibliography: books by Arthur C. Clarke	191

Foreword

All these stories were written during the quarter of a century that saw spaceflight transformed from a fantastic dream to an almost humdrum reality. Already it is very hard for me to realise that when I wrote *The Sentinel* in 1948, I never *really* believed that I would see a moon landing in my own lifetime. Still less did I imagine that, after six highly successful expeditions, we would abandon our satellite for at least a generation. . . .

The Sentinel, of course, is the story which twenty years later became the germ of Stanley Kubrick's *2001: A Space Odyssey*; elements from *Encounter in the Dawn* were also used in the screen-play. The idea that we might discover some relics of previous space visitors on the Moon or planets is now taken quite seriously by many scientists; unfortunately, false claims by incompetent or fraudulent writers have made it very difficult to conduct research in this area.

Yet even as I write these words, the radio astronomers are scratching their heads over some extremely powerful emissions which the Voyager space-probes appear to have detected in the rings of Saturn. Perhaps *something* has been parked there, waiting for us to discover it. If so, Stanley and I may have made a serious mistake in shifting the scene of action from Saturn—as in the original novel—to Jupiter, for the movie and the sequel *2010: Odyssey Two*. Time will tell, as it invariably does.

After producing over a hundred of them, it is now ten years since I wrote a short story, and I doubt if there will be any more. But I would not bet on it; unlike a novel (which is 99% perspiration) a short story can—occasionally—be 99% inspiration. Sometimes lightning strikes, and a few hours at the typewriter can produce the finished article. That happened in the case of *The Nine Billion Names of God*, which was the result of a wet weekend in New York; the view from my hotel room was so depressing that *any* alternative seemed better than reality— even the end of the world.

The Forgotten Enemy was also inspired by a glance out of the window—in this case, that of the micro-condominium at 88, Gray's Inn Road, London, which I shared from 1937 to 1940 with William F. Temple and the late Maurice K. Hanson. For those few pre-war years, it was the centre of British science-fiction fandom, as well as the headquarters of the fledgling British Interplanetary Society.

One weekend, during the last winter of peace, I was looking out across the roofs during a snowstorm and the horrid thought occurred to me: "Suppose it never stops snowing?" The re-sult—don't ask me why it took exactly ten years to get round to writing it—was *The Forgotten Enemy*. Until recently, I was a little embarrassed about the brief time-scale I had assumed for a major geological change. Now, I am reassured (?) to learn, many scientists believe that a new Ice Age could—indeed, *may*—come upon us with devastating swiftness implied in the story.

Incidentally, I must apologise for destroying the world no

less than five times in this volume. For a science-fiction writer
who calls himself an optimist, this seems a little excessive. But
at least *No Morning After* may be the only *humorous* story ever
written about the end of the world. I would be interested to
know if any other author has performed this dubious feat.

The technology described in *The Fires Within* now exists;
"acoustic holography" is being used to probe the upper layers
of the earth, and to produce images very much like those
described in the story. But not, I hope, *precisely* like them. . . .

An Ape About the House was written long before I had any
dealings with our closest relatives; now that I have met people
like Washoe and her associates I take the idea of *Pan sapiens*
quite seriously. For its further development, see the novel
Rendezvous with Rama and the short story *A Meeting with Medusa*
(in my 1972 collection, *The Wind From the Sun*).

I will let the other stories speak for themselves; if you like
them, I hope you may also enjoy their companions, in the five
earlier volumes, *Expedition to Earth*, *Reach for Tomorrow*, *Tales from
the "White Hart"*, *The Other Side of the Sky* and *Tales of Ten Worlds*.

Colombo, Sri Lanka
September 1982

The Nine Billion Names of God

"This is a slightly unusual request," said Dr. Wagner, with what he hoped was commendable restraint. "As far as I know, it's the first time anyone's been asked to supply a Tibetan monastery with an Automatic Sequence Computer. I don't wish to be inquisitive, but I should hardly have thought that your—ah—establishment had much use for such a machine. Could you explain just what you intend to do with it?"

"Gladly," replied the lama, readjusting his silk robes and carefully putting away the slide rule he had been using for currency conversions. "Your Mark V Computer can carry out any routine mathematical operation involving up to ten digits. However, for our work we are interested in *letters*, not numbers. As we wish you to modify the output circuits, the machine will be printing words, not columns of figures."

"I don't quite understand. . . ."

"This is a project on which we have been working for the last three centuries—since the lamasery was founded, in fact. It is somewhat alien to your way of thought, so I hope you will listen with an open mind while I explain it."

"Naturally."

"It is really quite simple. We have been compiling a list which shall contain all the possible names of God."

"I beg your pardon?"

"We have reason to believe," continued the lama imperturbably, "that all such names can be written with not more than nine letters in an alphabet we have devised."

"And you have been doing this for three centuries?"

"Yes: we expected it would take us about fifteen thousand years to complete the task."

"Oh," Dr. Wagner looked a little dazed. "Now I see why you wanted to hire one of our machines. But what exactly is the *purpose* of this project?"

The lama hesitated for a fraction of a second, and Wagner wondered if he had offended him. If so, there was no trace of annoyance in the reply.

"Call it ritual, if you like, but it's a fundamental part of our belief. All the many names of the Supreme Being—God, Jehova, Allah, and so on—they are only man-made labels. There is a philosophical problem of some difficulty here, which I do not propose to discuss, but somewhere among all the possible combinations of letters that can occur are what one may call the *real* names of God. By systematic permutation of letters, we have been trying to list them all."

"I see. You've been starting at AAAAAAA . . . and working up to ZZZZZZZ. . . ."

"Exactly—though we use a special alphabet of our own. Modifying the electromatic typewriters to deal with this is, of course, trivial. A rather more interesting problem is that of devising suitable circuits to eliminate ridiculous combinations. For example, no letter must occur more than three times in succession."

"Three? Surely you mean two."

"Three is correct: I am afraid it would take too long to explain why, even if you understood our language."

"I'm sure it would," said Wagner hastily. "Go on."

"Luckily, it will be a simple matter to adapt your Automatic Sequence Computer for this work, since once it has been programmed properly it will permute each letter in turn and print the result. What would have taken us fifteen thousand years it will be able to do in a hundred days."

Dr. Wagner was scarcely conscious of the faint sounds from the Manhattan streets far below. He was in a different world, a world of natural, not man-made, mountains. High up in their remote aeries these monks had been patiently at work, generation after generation, compiling their lists of meaningless words. Was there any limit to the follies of mankind? Still, he must give no hint of his inner thoughts. The customer was always right. . . .

"There's no doubt," replied the doctor, "that we can modify the Mark V to print lists of this nature. I'm much more worried about the problem of installation and maintenance. Getting out to Tibet, in these days, is not going to be easy."

"We can arrange that. The components are small enough to travel by air—that is one reason why we chose your machine. If you can get them to India, we will provide transport from there."

"And you want to hire two of our engineers?"

"Yes, for the three months that the project should occupy."

"I've no doubt that Personnel can manage that." Dr. Wagner scribbled a note on his desk pad. "There are just two other points—"

Before he could finish the sentence the lama had produced a small slip of paper.

"This is my certified credit balance at the Asiatic Bank."

13

"Thank you. It appears to be—ah—adequate. The second matter is so trivial that I hesitate to mention it—but it's surprising how often the obvious gets overlooked. What source of electrical energy have you?"

"A diesel generator providing fifty kilowatts at a hundred and ten volts. It was installed about five years ago and is quite reliable. It's made life at the lamasery much more comfortable, but of course it was really installed to provide power for the motors driving the prayer wheels."

"Of course," echoed Dr. Wagner. "I should have thought of that."

The view from the parapet was vertiginous, but in time one gets used to anything. After three months, George Hanley was not impressed by the two-thousand-foot swoop into the abyss or the remote checkerboard of fields in the valley below. He was leaning against the wind-smoothed stones and staring morosely at the distant mountains whose names he had never bothered to discover.

This, thought George, was the craziest thing that had ever happened to him. "Project Shangri-La," some wit back at the labs had christened it. For weeks now the Mark V had been churning out acres of sheets covered with gibberish. Patiently, inexorably, the computer had been rearranging letters in all their possible combinations, exhausting each class before going on to the next. As the sheets had emerged from the electromatic typewriters, the monks had carefully cut them up and pasted them into enormous books. In another week, heaven be praised, they would have finished. Just what obscure calculations had convinced the monks that they needn't bother to go on to words of ten, twenty, or a hundred letters, George didn't know. One of his recurring nightmares was that there would be some change of plan, and that the high lama (whom they'd naturally called Sam Jaffe, though he didn't look a bit like him) would suddenly announce that the project would be extended to approximately A.D. 2060. They were quite capable of it.

George heard the heavy wooden door slam in the wind as Chuck came out on to the parapet beside him. As usual, Chuck was smoking one of the cigars that made him so popular with the monks—who, it seemed, were quite willing to embrace all the minor and most of the major pleasures of life. That was one thing in their favour: they might be crazy, but they weren't bluenoses. Those frequent trips they took down to the village, for instance . . .

"Listen, George," said Chuck urgently. "I've learned something that means trouble."

"What's wrong? Isn't the machine behaving?" That was the worst contingency George could imagine. It might delay his return, and nothing could be more horrible. The way he felt now, even the sight of a TV commercial would seem like manna from heaven. At last it would be some link with home.

"No—it's nothing like that." Chuck settled himself on the parapet, which was unusual because normally he was scared of the drop. "I've just found what all this is about."

"What d'ya mean? I thought we knew."

"Sure—we know what the monks are trying to do. But we didn't know *why*. It's the craziest thing—"

"Tell me something new," growled George.

"—but old Sam's just come clean with me. You know the way he drops in every afternoon to watch the sheets roll out. Well, this time he seemed rather excited, or at least as near as he'll ever get to it. When I told him that we were on the last cycle he asked me, in that cute English accent of his, if I'd ever wondered what they were trying to do. I said, 'Sure'—and he told me."

"Go on: I'll buy it."

"Well, they believe that when they have listed all His names—and they reckon that there are about nine billion of them—God's purpose will be achieved. The human race will have finished what it was created to do, and there won't be any point in carrying on. Indeed, the very idea is something like blasphemy."

"Then what do they expect us to do? Commit suicide?"

"There's no need for that. When the list's completed, God steps in and simply winds things up . . . bingo!"

"Oh, I get it. When we finish our job, it will be the end of the world."

Chuck gave a nervous little laugh.

"That's just what I said to Sam. And do you know what happened? He looked at me in a very queer way, like I'd been stupid in class, and said, 'It's nothing as trivial as *that*.' "

George thought this over for a moment.

"That's what I call taking the Wide View," he said presently. "But what d'you suppose we should do about it? I don't see that it makes the slightest difference to us. After all, we already knew that they were crazy."

"Yes—but don't you see what may happen? When the list's complete and the Last Trump doesn't blow—or whatever it is they expect—*we* may get the blame. It's our machine they've been using. I don't like the situation one little bit."

"I see," said George slowly. "You've a point there. But this sort of thing's happened before, you know. When I was a kid down in Louisiana we had a crackpot preacher who once said the world was going to end next Sunday. Hundreds of people believed him—even sold their homes. Yet when nothing happened, they didn't turn nasty, as you'd expect. They just decided that he'd made a mistake in his calculations and went right on believing. I guess some of them still do."

"Well, this isn't Louisiana, in case you hadn't noticed. There are just two of us and hundreds of these monks. I like them, and I'll be sorry for old Sam when his lifework backfires on him. But all the same, I wish I was somewhere else."

"I've been wishing that for weeks. But there's nothing we can do until the contract's finished and the transport arrives to fly us out."

"Of course," said Chuck thoughtfully, "we could always try a bit of sabotage."

"Like hell we could! That would make things worse."

"Not the way I meant. Look at it like this. The machine will finish its run four days from now, on the present twenty-hours-a-day basis. The transport calls in a week. O.K.—then all we need to do is to find something that needs replacing during one of the overhaul periods—something that will hold up the works for a couple of days. We'll fix it, of course, but not too quickly. If we time matters properly, we can be down at the airfield when the last name pops out of the register. They won't be able to catch us then."

"I don't like it," said George. "It will be the first time I ever walked out on a job. Besides, it would make them suspicious. No, I'll sit tight and take what comes."

"I *still* don't like it," he said, seven days later, as the tough little mountain ponies carried them down the winding road. "And don't you think I'm running away because I'm afraid. I'm just sorry for those poor old guys up there, and I don't want to be around when they find what suckers they've been. Wonder how Sam will take it?"

"It's funny," replied Chuck, "but when I said goodbye I got the idea he knew we were walking out on him—and that he didn't care because he knew the machine was running smoothly and that the job would soon be finished. After that—well, of course, for him there just isn't any After That. . . ."

George turned in his saddle and stared back up the mountain road. This was the last place from which one could get a clear view of the lamasery. The squat, angular buildings were silhouetted against the afterglow of the sunset: here and there, lights gleamed like portholes in the side of an ocean liner. Electric lights, of course, sharing the same circuit as the Mark V. How much longer would they share it? wondered George. Would the monks smash up the computer in their rage and disappointment? Or would they just sit down quietly and begin their calculations all over again?

He knew exactly what was happening up on the mountain at this very moment. The high lama and his assistants would be sitting in their silk robes, inspecting the sheets as the junior monks carried them away from the typewriters and pasted them into the great volumes. No one would be saying anything. The only sound would be the incessant patter, the never-ending rainstorm of the keys hitting the paper, for the Mark V itself was utterly silent as it flashed through its thousands of calculations a second. Three months of this, thought George, was enough to start anyone climbing up the wall.

"There she is!" called Chuck, pointing down into the valley. "Ain't she beautiful!"

She certainly was, thought George. The battered old DC3 lay at the end of the runway like a tiny silver cross. In two hours she would be bearing them away to freedom and sanity. It was a thought worth savouring like a fine liqueur. George let it roll round his mind as the pony trudged patiently down the slope.

The swift night of the high Himalayas was now almost upon them. Fortunately, the road was very good, as roads went in that region, and they were both carrying torches. There was not the slightest danger, only a certain discomfort from the bitter cold. The sky overhead was perfectly clear, and ablaze with the familiar, friendly stars. At least there would be no risk, thought George, of the pilot being unable to take off because of weather conditions. That had been his only remaining worry.

He began to sing, but gave it up after a while. This vast arena of mountains, gleaming like whitely hooded ghosts on every side, did not encourage such ebullience. Presently George glanced at his watch.

"Should be there in an hour," he called back over his shoulder to Chuck. Then he added, in an afterthought: "Wonder if the computer's finished its run. It was due about now."

Chuck didn't reply, so George swung round in his saddle. He could just see Chuck's face, a white oval turned towards the sky.

"Look," whispered Chuck, and George lifted his eyes to heaven. (There is always a last time for everything.)

Overhead, without any fuss, the stars were going out.

An Ape About the House

Granny thought it a perfectly horrible idea; but then, she could remember the days when there were *human* servants.

"If you imagine," she snorted, "that I'll share the house with a monkey, you're very much mistaken."

"Don't be so old-fashioned," I answered. "Anyway, Dorcas isn't a monkey."

"Then what is she—it?"

I flipped through the pages of the Biological Engineering Corporation's guide. "Listen to this, Gran," I said. " 'The Superchimp (Registered Trade-mark) *Pan Sapiens* is an intelligent anthropoid, derived by selective breeding and genetic modification from basic chimpanzee stock—' "

"Just what I said! A monkey!"

" '—and with a large-enough vocabulary to understand simple orders. It can be trained to perform all types of domestic work or routine manual labour and is docile, affectionate, housebroken, and particularly good with children—' "

"Children! Would you trust Johnnie and Susan with a—a *gorilla*?"

I put the handbook down with a sigh.

"You've got a point there. Dorcas *is* expensive, and if I find the little monsters knocking her about—"

At this moment, fortunately, the door buzzer sounded. "Sign, please," said the delivery man. I signed, and Dorcas entered our lives.

"Hello, Dorcas," I said. "I hope you'll be happy here."

Her big, mournful eyes peered out at me from beneath their heavy ridges. I'd met much uglier humans, though she was rather an odd shape, being only about four feet tall and very nearly as wide. In her neat, plain uniform she looked just like a maid from one of those early twentieth-century movies; her feet, however, were bare and covered an astonishing amount of floor space.

"Morning, Ma'am," she answered, in slurred but perfectly intelligible accents.

"She can speak!" squawked Granny.

"Of course," I answered. "She can pronounce over fifty words, and can understand two hundred. She'll learn more as she grows used to us, but for the moment we must stick to the vocabulary on pages forty-two and forty-three of the handbook." I passed the instruction manual over to Granny; for once, she couldn't find even a single word to express *her* feelings.

Dorcas settled down very quickly. Her basic training—Class A Domestic, plus Nursery Duties—had been excellent, and by the end of the first month there were very few jobs around the house that she couldn't do, from laying the table to changing the children's clothes. At first she had an annoying habit of picking up things with her feet; it seemed as natural to her as using her hands, and it took a long time to break her of it. One of Granny's cigarette butts finally did the trick.

She was good-natured, conscientious, and didn't answer back.

Of course, she was not terribly bright, and some jobs had to be explained to her at great length before she got the point. It took several weeks before I discovered her limitations and allowed for them; at first it was quite hard to remember that she was not exactly human, and that it was no good engaging her in the sort of conversations we women occupy ourselves with when we get together. Or not many of them; she did have an interest in clothes, and was fascinated by colours. If I'd let her dress the way she wanted, she'd have looked like a refugee from Mardi Gras.

The children, I was relieved to find, adored her. I know what people say about Johnnie and Sue, and admit that it contains some truth. It's so hard to bring up children when their father's away most of the time, and to make matters worse, Granny spoils them when I'm not looking. So indeed does Eric, whenever his ship's on Earth, and I'm left to cope with the resulting tantrums. Never marry a spaceman if you can possibly avoid it; the pay may be good, but the glamour soon wears off.

By the time Eric got back from the Venus run, with three weeks' accumulated leave, our new maid had settled down as one of the family. Eric took her in his stride; after all, he'd met much odder creatures on the planets. He grumbled about the expense, of course, but I pointed out that now that so much of the housework was taken off my hands, we'd be able to spend more time together and do some of the visiting that had proved impossible in the past. I looked forward to having a little social life again, now that Dorcas could take care of the children.

For there was plenty of social life at Port Goddard, even though we were stuck in the middle of the Pacific. (Ever since what happened to Miami, of course, all major launching sites have been a long, long way from civilization.) There was a constant flow of distinguished visitors and travellers from all parts of the Earth—not to mention remoter points.

Every community has its arbiter of fashion and culture, its *grande dame* who is resented yet copied by all her unsuccessful rivals. At Port Goddard it was Christine Swanson; her husband was Commodore of the Space Service, and she never let us forget it. Whenever a liner touched down, she would invite all the officers on Base to a reception at her stylishly antique nineteenth-century mansion. It was advisable to go, unless you had a very good excuse, even though that meant looking at Christine's paintings. She fancied herself as an artist, and the walls were hung with multicoloured daubs. Thinking of polite remarks to make about them was one of the major hazards of Christine's parties; another was her metre-long cigarette holder.

There was a new batch of paintings since Eric had been away: Christine had entered her "square" period. "You see, my dears," she explained to us, "the old-fashioned oblong pictures are terribly dated—they just don't go with the Space Age. There's no such thing as up or down, horizontal or vertical out *there*, so no really modern picture should have one side longer than another. And ideally, it should look *exactly* the same whichever way you hang it—I'm working on that right now."

"That seems very logical," said Eric tactfully. (After all, the Commodore was his boss.) But when our hostess was out of earshot, he added, "I don't know if Christine's pictures are hung the right way up, but I'm sure they're hung the wrong side to the wall."

I agreed; before I got married I spent several years at an art school and considered I knew something about the subject.

Given as much cheek as Christine, I could have made quite a hit with my own canvases, which were now gathering dust in the garage.

"You know, Eric," I said a little cattily, "I could teach Dorcas to paint better than this."

He laughed and answered, "It might be fun to try it some day, if Christine gets out of hand." Then I forgot all about the matter—until a month later, when Eric was back in space.

The exact cause of the fight isn't important; it arose over a community development scheme on which Christine and I took opposing viewpoints. She won, as usual, and I left the meeting breathing fire and brimstone. When I got home, the first thing I saw was Dorcas, looking at the coloured pictures in one of the weeklies—and I remembered Eric's words.

I put down my handbag, took off my hat, and said firmly: "Dorcas—come out to the garage."

It took some time to dig out my oils and easel from under the pile of discarded toys, old Christmas decorations, skindiving gear, empty packing cases, and broken tools (it seemed that Eric never had time to tidy up before he shot off into space again). There were several unfinished canvases buried among the debris, which would do for a start. I set up a landscape which had got as far as one skinny tree, and said: "Now Dorcas—I'm going to teach you to paint."

My plan was simple and not altogether honest. Although apes had, of course, splashed paint on canvas often enough in the past, none of them had created a genuine, properly composed work of art. I was sure that Dorcas couldn't either, but no one need know that mine was the guiding hand. She could get all the credit.

I was not actually going to lie to anyone, however. Though I would create the design, mix the pigments, and do most of the execution, I would let Dorcas tackle just as much of the work as she could handle. I hoped that she could fill in the areas of solid colour, and perhaps develop a characteristic style of brushwork in the process. With any luck, I estimated, she might be able to do perhaps a quarter of the actual work. Then I could claim it was all hers with a reasonably clear conscience—for hadn't Michelangelo and Leonardo signed paintings that were largely done by their assistants? I'd be Dorcas' "assistant".

I must confess that I was a little disappointed. Though Dorcas quickly got the general idea, and soon understood the use of brush and palette, her execution was very clumsy. She seemed unable to make up her mind which hand to use, but kept transferring the brush from one to the other. In the end I had to do almost all the work, and she merely contributed a few dabs of paint.

Still, I could hardly expect her to become a master in a couple of lessons, and it was really of no importance. If Dorcas was an artistic flop, I would just have to stretch the truth a little farther when I claimed that it was all her own work.

I was in no hurry; this was not the sort of thing that could be rushed. At the end of a couple of months, the School of Dorcas had produced a dozen paintings, all of them on carefully chosen themes that would be familiar to a Superchimp at Port Goddard. There was a study of the lagoon, a view of our house, an impression of a night launching (all glare and explosions of light), a fishing scene, a palm grove—clichés, of course, but anything else would rouse suspicion. Before she came to us, I don't suppose Dorcas had seen much of the world outside the labs where she had been reared and trained.

The best of these paintings (and some of them *were* good— after all, I should know) I hung around the house in places where my friends could hardly fail to notice them. Everything worked perfectly; admiring queries were followed by astonished cries of "You don't say!" when I modestly disclaimed responsibility. There was some scepticism, but I soon demolished that by letting a few privileged friends see Dorcas at work. I chose the viewers for their ignorance of art, and the picture was an abstraction in red, gold, and black which no one dared to criticize. By this time, Dorcas could fake it quite well, like a movie actor pretending to play a musical instrument.

Just to spread the news around, I gave away some of the best paintings, pretending that I considered them no more than amusing novelties—yet at the same time giving just the barest hint of jealousy. "I've hired Dorcas," I said testily, "to work for me—not for the Museum of Modern Art." And I was *very* careful not to draw any comparisons between her paintings and those of Christine: our mutual friends could be relied upon to do that.

When Christine came to see me, ostensibly to discuss our quarrel "like two sensible people", I knew that she was on the run. So I capitulated gracefully as we took tea in the drawing room, beneath one of Dorcas' most impressive productions. (Full moon rising over the lagoon—very cold, blue, and mysterious. I was really quite proud of it.) There was not a word about the picture, or about Dorcas; but Christine's eyes told me all I wanted to know. The next week, an exhibition she had been planning was quietly cancelled.

Gamblers say that you should quit when you're ahead of the game. If I had stopped to think, I should have known that Christine would not let the matter rest there. Sooner or later, she was bound to counter-attack.

She chose her time well, waiting until the kids were at

school, Granny was away visiting, and I was at the shopping centre on the other side of the island. Probably she phoned first to check that no one was at home—no one human, that is. We had told Dorcas not to answer calls; though she'd done so in the early days, it had not been a success. A Superchimp on the phone sounds exactly like a drunk, and this can lead to all sorts of complications.

I can reconstruct the whole sequence of events: Christine must have driven up to the house, expressed acute disappointment at my absence, and invited herself in. She would have wasted no time in getting to work on Dorcas, but luckily I'd taken the precaution of briefing my anthropoid colleague. "Dorcas make," I'd said, over and over again, each time one of our productions was finished. "Not Missy make—*Dorcas* make." And, in the end, I'm sure she believed this herself.

If my brainwashing, and the limitations of a fifty-word vocabulary, baffled Christine, she did not stay baffled for long. She was a lady of direct action, and Dorcas was a docile and obedient soul. Christine, determined to expose fraud and collusion, must have been gratified by the promptness with which she was led into the garage studio; she must also have been just a little surprised.

I arrived home about half an hour later, and knew that there was trouble afoot as soon as I saw Christine's car parked at the kerb. I could only hope I was in time, but as soon as I stepped into the uncannily silent house, I realized that it was too late. *Something* had happened; Christine would surely be talking, even if she had only an ape as audience. To her, any silence was as great a challenge as a blank canvas; it had to be filled with the sound of her own voice.

The house was utterly still; there was no sign of life. With a sense of mounting apprehension, I tiptoed through the drawing room, the dining room, the kitchen, and out into the back. The garage door was open, and I peered cautiously through.

It was a bitter moment of truth. Finally freed from my influence, Dorcas had at last developed a style of her own. She was swiftly and confidently painting—but not in the way *I* had so carefully taught her. And as for her subject . . .

I was deeply hurt when I saw the caricature that was giving Christine such obvious enjoyment. After all that I had done for Dorcas, this seemed sheer ingratitude. Of course, I know now that no malice was involved, and that she was merely expressing herself. The psychologists, and the critics who wrote those absurd programme notes for her exhibition at the Guggenheim, say that her portraits cast a vivid light on man-animal relationships, and allow us to look for the first time at the human race from outside. But I did not see it *that* way when I ordered Dorcas back into the kitchen.

For the subject was not the only thing that upset me: what really rankled was the thought of all the time I had wasted improving her technique—and her manners. She was ignoring everything I had ever told her, as she sat in front of the easel with her arms folded motionless on her chest.

Even then, at the very beginning of her career as an independent artist, it was painfully obvious that Dorcas had more talent in either of her swiftly moving feet than I had in both my hands.

Green Fingers

I am very sorry, now that it's too late, that I never got to know Vladimir Surov. As I remember him, he was a quiet little man who could understand English but couldn't speak it well enough to make conversation. Even to his colleagues, I suspect he was a bit of an enigma. Whenever I went aboard the *Ziolkovski*, he would be sitting in a corner working on his notes or peering through a microscope, a man who clung to his privacy even in the tight and tiny world of a spaceship. The rest of the crew did not seem to mind his aloofness; when they spoke to him, it was clear that they regarded him with tolerant affection, as well as with respect. That was hardly surprising; the work he had done developing plants and trees that could flourish far inside the Arctic Circle had already made him the most famous botanist in Russia.

The fact that the Russian expedition had taken a botanist to the moon had caused a good deal of amusement, though it was really no odder than the fact that there were biologists on both the British and American ships. During the years before the first lunar landing, a good deal of evidence had accumulated hinting that some form of vegetation might exist on the moon, despite its airlessness and lack of water. The president of the U.S.S.R. Academy of Science was one of the leading proponents of this theory, and being too old to make the trip himself had done the next best thing by sending Surov.

The complete absence of any such vegetation, living or fossil, in the thousand or so square miles explored by our various parties was the first big disappointment the moon had reserved for us. Even those sceptics who were quite certain that no form of life could exist on the moon would have been very glad to have been proved wrong—as of course they were, five years later, when Richards and Shannon made their astonishing discovery inside the great walled plain of Eratosthenes. But *that* revelation still lay in the future; at the time of the first landing, it seemed that Surov had come to the moon in vain.

He did not appear unduly depressed, but kept himself as busy as the rest of the crew studying soil samples and looking after the little hydroponic farm whose pressurized, transparent tubes formed a gleaming network around the *Ziolkovski*. Neither we nor the Americans had gone in for this sort of thing, having calculated that it was better to ship food from Earth than to grow it on the spot—at least until the time came to set up a permanent base. We were right in terms of economics, but wrong in terms of morale. The tiny airtight greenhouses inside which Surov grew his vegetables and dwarf fruit trees were an oasis upon which we often feasted our eyes when we had grown tired of the immense desolation surrounding us.

One of the many disadvantages of being commander was that I seldom had much chance to do any active exploring; I was too busy preparing reports for Earth, checking stores, arranging programmes and duty rosters, conferring with my opposite numbers in the American and Russian ships, and trying—not always successfully—to guess what would go wrong next. As a result, I sometimes did not go outside the base for two or three days at a time, and it was a standing joke that my space suit was a haven for moths.

Perhaps it is because of this that I can remember all my trips outside so vividly; certainly I can recall my only encounter with Surov. It was near noon, with the sun high above the southern mountains and the new Earth a barely visible thread of silver a few degrees away from it. Henderson, our geo-physicist, wanted to take some magnetic readings at a series of check points a couple of miles to the east of the base. Every-one else was busy, and I was momentarily on top of my work, so we set off together on foot.

The journey was not long enough to merit taking one of the scooters, especially because the charges in the batteries were getting low. In any case, I always enjoyed walking out in the open on the moon. It was not merely the scenery, which even at its most awe-inspiring one can grow accustomed to after a while. No—what I never tired of was the effortless, slow-motion way in which every step took me bounding over the landscape, giving me the freedom that before the coming of space flight men only knew in dreams.

We had done the job and were halfway home when I noticed a figure moving across the plain about a mile to the south of us—not far, in fact, from the Russian base. I snapped my field glasses down inside my helmet and took a careful look at the other explorer. Even at close range, of course, you can't identify a man in a space suit, but because the suits are always coded by colour and number that makes no practical difference.

31

"Who is it?" asked Henderson over the short-range radio channel to which we were both tuned.

"Blue suit, Number 3—that would be Surov. But I don't understand. *He's by himself.*"

It is one of the most fundamental rules of lunar exploration that no one goes anywhere alone on the surface of the moon. So many accidents can happen, which would be trivial if you were with a companion—but fatal if you were by yourself. How would you manage, for example, if your space suit developed a slow leak in the small of the back and you couldn't put on a repair patch? That may sound funny; but it's happened.

"Perhaps his buddy has had an accident and he's going to fetch help," suggested Henderson. "Maybe we had better call him."

I shook my head. Surov was obviously in no hurry. He had been out on a trip of his own, and was making his leisurely way back to the *Ziolkovski*. It was no concern of mine if Commander Krasnin let his people go out on solo trips, though it seemed a deplorable practice. And if Surov was breaking regulations, it was equally no concern of mine to report him.

During the next two months, my men often spotted Surov making his lone way over the landscape, but he always avoided them if they got too near. I made some discreet inquiries, and found that Commander Krasnin had been forced, owing to shortage of men, to relax some of his safety rules. But I couldn't find out what Surov was up to, though I never dreamed that his commander was equally in the dark.

It was with an "I told you so" feeling that I got Krasnin's emergency call. We had all had men in trouble before and had had to send out help, but this was the first time anyone had been lost and had not replied when his ship had sent out the recall signal. There was a hasty radio conference, a line of action was drawn up, and search parties fanned out from each of the three ships.

Once again I was with Henderson, and it was only common sense for us to backtrack along the route that we had seen Surov following. It was in what we regarded as "our" territory, quite some distance away from Surov's own ship, and as we scrambled up the low foot-hills it occurred to me for the first time that the Russian might have been doing something he wanted to keep from his colleagues. What it might be, I could not imagine.

Henderson found him, and yelled for help over his suit radio. But it was much too late; Surov was lying, face down, his deflated suit crumpled around him. He had been kneeling when something had smashed the plastic globe of his helmet; you could see how he had pitched forward and died instantaneously.

When Commander Krasnin reached us, we were still staring at the unbelievable object that Surov had been examining when he died. It was about three feet high, a leathery, greenish oval rooted to the rocks with a wide-spread network of tendrils. Yes—rooted; for it was a plant. A few yards away were two others, much smaller and apparently dead, since they were blackened and withered.

My first reaction was: "So there *is* life on the moon, after all!" It was not until Krasnin's voice spoke in my ears that I realized how much more marvellous was the truth.

"Poor Vladimir!" he said. "We knew he was a genius, yet we laughed at him when he told us of his dream. So he kept his greatest work a secret. He conquered the Arctic with his hybrid wheat, but *that* was only a beginning. He has brought life to the moon—and death as well."

As I stood there, in that first moment of astonished revelation, it still seemed a miracle. Today, all the world knows the history of "Surov's cactus", as it was inevitably if quite inaccurately christened, and it has lost much of its wonder. His notes have told the full story, and have described the years of experimentation that finally led him to a plant whose leathery skin would enable it to survive in vacuum, and whose far-ranging, acid-secreting roots would enable it to grow upon rocks where even lichens would be hard put to thrive. And we have seen the realization of the second stage of Surov's dream, for the cactus which will forever bear his name has already broken up vast areas of the lunar rock and so prepared a way for the more specialized plants that now feed every human being upon the moon.

Krasnin bent down beside the body of his colleague and lifted it effortlessly against the low gravity. He fingered the shattered fragments of the plastic helmet, and shook his head in perplexity.

"What could have happened to him?" he said. "It almost looks as if the plant did it, but that's ridiculous."

The green enigma stood there on the no-longer barren plain, tantalizing us with its promise and its mystery. Then Henderson said slowly, as if thinking aloud:

"I believe I've got the answer; I've just remembered some of the botany I did at school. If Surov designed this plant for lunar conditions, how would he arrange for it to propagate itself? The seeds would have to be scattered over a very wide area in the hope of finding a few suitable places to grow. There are no birds or animals here to carry them, in the way that happens on Earth. I can only think of one solution—and some of our terrestrial plants have already used it."

He was interrupted by my yell. Something had hit with a

34

resounding clang against the metal waistband of my suit. It did no damage, but it was so sudden and unexpected that it took me utterly by surprise.

A seed lay at my feet, about the size and shape of a plum stone. A few yards away, we found the one that had shattered Surov's helmet as he bent down. He must have known that the plant was ripe, but in his eagerness to examine it he had forgotten what that implied. I have seen a cactus throw its seed a quarter of a mile under the low lunar gravity. Surov had been shot at point-blank range by his own creation.

Trouble with the Natives

The flying saucer came down vertically through the clouds, braked to a halt about fifty feet from the ground, and settled with a considerable bump on a patch of heather-strewn moorland.

"That," said Captain Wyxtpthll, "was a lousy landing." He did not, of course, use precisely these words. To human ears his remarks would have sounded rather like the clucking of an angry hen. Master Pilot Krtclugg unwound three of his tentacles from the control panel, stretched all four of his legs, and relaxed comfortably.

"Not my fault the automatics have packed up again," he grumbled. "But what do you expect with a ship that should have been scrapped five thousand years ago? If those cheese-paring form-fillers back at Base Planet—"

"Oh, all right! We're down in one piece, which is more than I expected. Tell Crysteel and Danstor to come in here. I want a word with them before they go."

Crysteel and Danstor were, very obviously, of a different species from the rest of the crew. They had only one pair of legs and arms, no eyes at the back of the head, and other physical deficiencies which their colleagues did their best to overlook. These very defects, however, had made them the obvious choice for this particular mission, for it had needed only a minimum of disguise to let them pass as human beings under all but the closest scrutiny.

"Now you're perfectly sure," said the Captain, "that you understand your instructions?"

"Of course," said Crysteel, slightly huffed. "This isn't the first time I've made contact with a primitive race. My training in anthropology—"

"Good. And the language?"

"Well, that's Danstor's business, but I can speak it reasonably fluently now. It's a very simple language and after all we've been studying their radio programmes for a couple of years."

"Any other points before you go?"

"Er—there's just one matter." Crysteel hesitated slightly. "It's quite obvious from their broadcasts that the social system is very primitive, and that crime and lawlessness are widespread. Many of the wealthier citizens have to use what are called 'detectives' or 'special agents' to protect their lives and property. Now we know it's against regulations, but we were wondering . . ."

"What?"

"Well, we'd feel much safer if we could take a couple of Mark III disrupters with us."

"Not on your life! I'd be court-martialled if they heard about it at the Base. Suppose you killed some of the natives— then I'd have the Bureau of Interstellar Politics, the Aborigines Conservancy Board, and half a dozen others after me."

"There'd be just as much trouble if *we* got killed," Crysteel pointed out with considerable emotion. "After all, you're responsible for our safety. Remember that radio play I was telling you about? It described a typical household, but there were two murders in the first half hour!"

"Oh, very well. But only a Mark II—we don't want you to do too much damage if there *is* trouble."

"Thanks a lot; that's a great relief. I'll report every thirty minutes as arranged. We shouldn't be gone more than a couple of hours."

Captain Wyxtpthll watched them disappear over the brow of the hill. He sighed deeply.

"Why," he said, "of all the people in the ship did it have to be *those* two?"

"It couldn't be helped," answered the pilot. "All these primitive races are terrified of anything strange. If they saw *us* coming, there'd be general panic and before we knew where we were the bombs would be falling on top of us. You just can't rush these things."

Captain Wyxtpthll was absentmindedly making a cat's cradle out of his tentacles in the way he did when he was worried.

"Of course," he said, "if they don't come back I can always go away and report the place dangerous." He brightened considerably. "Yes, that would save a lot of trouble."

"And waste all the months we've spent studying it?" said the pilot, scandalized. "They won't be wasted," replied the captain, unravelling himself with a flick that no human eye could have followed. "Our report will be useful for the next survey ship. I'll suggest that we make another visit in—oh, let's say five thousand years. By then the place may be civilized— though frankly, I doubt it."

Samuel Higginsbotham was settling down to a snack of cheese and cider when he saw the two figures approaching along the lane. He wiped his mouth with the back of his hand, put the bottle carefully down beside his hedge-trimming tools, and stared with mild surprise at the couple as they came into range.

"Mornin'," he said cheerfully between mouthfuls of cheese.

The strangers paused. One was surreptitiously ruffling through a small book which, if Sam only knew, was packed with such common phrases and expressions as: "Before the weather forecast, here is a gale warning," "Stick 'em up—I've got you covered!", and "Calling all cars!" Danstor, who had no needs for these aids to memory, replied promptly enough.

"Good morning my man," he said in his best B.B.C. accent. "Could you direct us to the nearest hamlet, village, small town or other such civilized community?"

"Eh?" said Sam. He peered suspiciously at the strangers, aware for the first time that there was something very odd about their clothes. One did not, he realized dimly, normally wear a roll-top sweater with a smart pin-striped suit of the pattern fancied by city gents. And the fellow who was still fussing with the little book was actually wearing full evening dress which would have been faultless but for the lurid green and red tie, the hob-nailed boots and the cloth cap. Crysteel and Danstor had done their best, but they had seen too many television plays. When one considers that they had no other source of information, their sartorial aberrations were at least understandable.

Sam scratched his head. Furriners, I suppose, he told himself. Not even the townsfolk got themselves up like this.

He pointed down the road and gave them explicit directions in an accent so broad that no one residing outside the range of the B.B.C.'s West Regional transmitter could have understood more than one word in three. Crysteel and Danstor, whose home planet was so far away that Marconi's first signals couldn't possibly have reached it yet, did even worse than this. But they managed to get the general idea and retired in good order, both wondering if their knowledge of English was as good as they had believed.

So came and passed, quite uneventfully and without record in the history books, the first meeting between humanity and beings from Outside.

"I suppose," said Danstor thoughtfully, but without much conviction, "that he wouldn't have done? It would have saved us a lot of trouble."

"I'm afraid not. Judging by his clothes, and the work he was obviously engaged upon, he could not have been a very intelligent or valuable citizen. I doubt if he could even have understood who we were."

"Here's another one!" said Danstor, pointing ahead.

"Don't make sudden movements that might cause alarm. Just walk along naturally, and let him speak first."

The man ahead strode purposefully towards them, showed not the slightest signs of recognition, and before they had recovered was already disappearing into the distance.

"Well!" said Danstor.

"It doesn't matter," replied Crysteel philosophically. "He probably wouldn't have been any use either."

"That's no excuse for bad manners!"

They gazed with some indignation at the retreating back of Professor Fitzsimmons as, wearing his oldest hiking outfit and engrossed in a difficult piece of atomic theory, he dwindled down the lane. For the first time, Crysteel began to suspect uneasily that it might not be as simple to make contact as he had optimistically believed.

Little Milton was a typical English village, nestling at the

foot of the hills whose higher slopes now concealed so porten-
tous a secret. There were very few people about on this summer
morning, for the men were already at work and the women-
folk were still tidying up after the exhausting task of getting
their lords and masters safely out of the way. Consequently
Crysteel and Danstor had almost reached the centre of the
village before their first encounter, which happened to be with
the village postman, cycling back to the office after completing
his rounds. He was in a very bad temper, having had to deliver
a penny postcard to Dodgson's farm, a couple of miles off his
normal route. In addition, the weekly parcel of laundry which
Gunner Evans sent home to his doting mother had been a
lot heavier than usual, as well it might, since it contained four
tins of bully beef pinched from the cookhouse.

"Excuse me," said Danstor politely.

"Can't stop," said the postman, in no mood for casual
conversation. "Got another round to do." Then he was
gone.

"This is really the limit!" protested Danstor. "Are they *all*
going to be like this?"

"You've simply got to be patient," said Crysteel. "Remember
their customs are quite different from ours; it may take some
time to gain their confidence. I've had this sort of trouble with
primitive races before. Every anthropologist has to get used
to it."

"Hmm," said Danstor. "I suggest that we call at some of
their houses. Then they won't be able to run away."

"Very well," agreed Crysteel doubtfully. "But avoid anything that looks like a religious shrine, otherwise we may get
into trouble."

Old Widow Tomkins' council-house could hardly have
been mistaken, even by the most inexperienced of explorers,

41

for such an object. The old lady was agreeably excited to see two gentlemen standing on her doorstep, and noticed nothing at all odd about their clothes. Visions of unexpected legacies, of newspaper reporters asking about her 100th birthday (she was really only 95, but had managed to keep it dark) flashed through her mind. She picked up the slate she kept hanging by the door and went gaily to forth greet her visitors.

"You'll have to write it down," she simpered, holding out the slate. "I've been deaf this last twenty years."

Crysteel and Danstor looked at each other in dismay. This was a completely unexpected snag, for the only written characters they had ever seen were television programme announcements, and they had never fully deciphered those. But Danstor, who had an almost photographic memory, rose to the occasion. Holding the chalk very awkwardly, he wrote a sentence which, he had reason to believe, was in common use during such breakdowns in communication.

As her mysterious visitors walked sadly away, old Mrs. Tomkins stared in baffled bewilderment at the marks on her slate. It was some time before she deciphered the characters— Danstor had made several mistakes—and even then she was little the wiser.

TRANSMISSIONS WILL BE RESUMED AS
SOON AS POSSIBLE.

It was the best that Danstor could do; but the old lady never did get to the bottom of it.

They were little luckier at the next house they tried. The door was answered by a young lady whose vocabulary consisted largely of giggles, and who eventually broke down completely and slammed the door in their faces. As they listened to the muffled, hysterical laughter, Crysteel and Danstor began to suspect, with sinking hearts, that their disguise as normal human beings was not as effective as they had intended.

At Number 3, on the other hand, Mrs. Smith was only too willing to talk—at 120 words to the minute in an accent as impenetrable as Sam Higginsbotham's. Danstor made his apologies as soon as he could get a word in edgeways, and moved on.

"Doesn't *anyone* talk as they do on the radio?" he lamented. "How do they understand their own programmes if they all speak like this?"

"I think we must have landed in the wrong place," said Crysteel, even his optimism beginning to fail. It sagged still further when he had been mistaken, in swift succession, for a Gallup Poll investigator, the prospective Conservative candidate, a vacuum-cleaner salesman, and a dealer from the local black market.

At the sixth or seventh attempt they ran out of housewives. The door was opened by a gangling youth who clutched in one clammy paw an object which at once hypnotized the visitors. It was a magazine whose cover displayed a giant rocket climbing upward from a crater-studded planet which, whatever it might be, was obviously not the Earth. Across the background were the words: "Staggering Stories of Pseudo-Science. Price 25 cents."

Crysteel looked at Danstor with a "Do you think what I think?" expression which the other returned. Here at last, surely, was someone who could understand them. His spirits mounting, Danstor addressed the youngster.

"I think you can help us, " he said politely. "We find it very difficult to make ourselves understood here. You see, we've just landed on this planet from space and we want to get in touch with your government."

"Oh," said Jimmy Williams, not yet fully returned to Earth

from his vicarious adventures among the outer moons of Saturn. "Where's your spaceship?"

"It's up in the hills; we didn't want to frighten anyone."

"Is it a rocket?"

"Good gracious no. They've been obsolete for thousands of years."

"Then how does it work? Does it use atomic power?"

"I suppose so," said Danstor, who was pretty shaky on physics. "Is there any other kind of power?"

"This is getting us nowhere," said Crysteel, impatient for once. "We've got to ask *him* questions. Try and find where there are some officials we can meet."

Before Danstor could answer, a stentorian voice came from inside the house.

"Jimmy! Who's there?"

"Two . . . men," said Jimmy, a little doubtfully. "At least, they look like men. They've come from Mars. I always said that was going to happen."

There was the sound of ponderous movements, and a lady of elephantine bulk and ferocious mien appeared from the gloom. She glared at the strangers, looked at the magazine Jimmy was carrying, and summed up the situation.

"You ought to be ashamed of yourselves!" she cried, rounding on Crysteel and Danstor. "It's bad enough having a good-for-nothing son in the house who wastes all his time reading this rubbish, without grown men coming along putting more ideas into his head. Men from Mars, indeed! I suppose you've come in one of those flying saucers!"

"But I never mentioned Mars," protested Danstor feebly.

Slam! From behind the door came the sound of violent altercation, the unmistakable noise of tearing paper, and a wail of anguish. And that was that.

"Well," said Danstor at last. "What do we try next? And why did he say we came from Mars? That isn't even the nearest planet, if I remember correctly."

"I don't know," said Crysteel. "But I suppose it's natural for them to assume that we come from some close planet. They're going to have a shock when they find out the truth. Mars, indeed! That's even worse than here, from the reports I've seen." He was obviously beginning to lose some of his scientific detachment.

"Let's leave the houses for a while," said Danstor. "There must be some more people outside."

This statement proved to be perfectly true, for they had not gone much further before they found themselves surrounded by small boys making incomprehensible but obviously rude remarks.

"Should we try and placate them with gifts?" said Danstor anxiously. "That usually works among more backward races."

"Well, have you brought any?"

"No I thought you—"

Before Danstor could finish, their tormentors took to their heels and disappeared down a side street. Coming along the road was a majestic figure in a blue uniform.

Crysteel's eyes lit up.

"A policeman!" he said. "Probably going to investigate a murder somewhere. But perhaps he'll spare us a minute," he added, not very hopefully.

P.C. Hinks eyed the strangers with some astonishment, but managed to keep his feelings out of his voice.

"Hello, gents. Looking for anything?"

"As a matter of fact, yes," said Danstor in his friendliest and most soothing tone of voice. "Perhaps you can help us. You see, we've just landed on this planet and want to make contact with the authorities."

"Eh?" said P.C. Hinks startled. There was a long pause—though not too long, for P.C. Hinks was a bright young man who had no intention of remaining a village constable all his life. "So you've just landed, have you? In a spaceship, I suppose?"

"That's right," said Danstor, immensely relieved at the absence of the incredulity, or even violence, which such announcements all too often provoked on the more primitive planets.

"Well, well!" said P.C. Hinks, in tones which he hoped would inspire confidence and feelings of amity. (Not that it mattered much if they both became violent—they seemed a pretty skinny pair.) "Just tell me what you want, and I'll see what we can do about it."

"I'm so glad," said Danstor. "You see, we've landed in this rather remote spot because we don't want to create a panic. It would be best to keep our presence known to as few people as possible until we have contacted your government."

"I quite understand," replied P.C. Hinks, glancing round hastily to see if there was anyone through whom he could send a message to his sergeant. "And what do you propose to do then?"

"I'm afraid I can't discuss our long-term policy with regard to Earth," said Danstor cagily. "All I can say is that this section of the Universe is being surveyed and opened up for development, and we're quite sure we can help you in many ways."

"That's very nice of you," said P.C. Hinks heartily. "I think the best thing is for you to come along to the station with me so that we can put through a call to the Prime Minister."

"Thank you very much," said Danstor, full of gratitude. They walked trustingly beside P.C. Hinks, despite his slight tendency to keep behind them, until they reached the village police station.

"This way, gents," said P.C. Hinks, politely ushering them into a room which was really rather poorly lit and not at all well furnished, even by the somewhat primitive standards they had expected. Before they could fully take in their surroundings, there was a "click" and they found themselves separated from their guide by a large door composed entirely of iron bars.

"Now don't worry," said P.C. Hinks. "Everything will be quite all right. I'll be back in a minute."

Crysteel and Danstor gazed at each other with a surmise that rapidly deepened to a dreadful certainty.

"We're locked in!"

"This is a prison!"

"Now what are we going to do?"

"I don't know if you chaps understand English," said a languid voice from the gloom, "but you might let a fellow sleep in peace."

For the first time, the two prisoners saw that they were not alone. Lying on a bed in the corner of the cell was a somewhat dilapidated young man, who gazed at them blearily out of one resentful eye.

"My goodness!" said Danstor nervously. "Do you suppose he's a dangerous criminal?"

"He doesn't look very dangerous at the moment," said Crysteel, with more accuracy than he guessed.

"What are *you* in for, anyway?" asked the stranger, sitting up unsteadily. "You look as if you've been to a fancy-dress party. Oh, my poor head!" He collapsed again into the prone position.

47

"Fancy locking up anyone as ill as this!" said Danstor, who was a kind-hearted individual. Then he continued, in English, "I don't know why we're here. We just told the policeman who we were and where we came from, and this is what's happened."

"Well, who are you?"

"We've just landed—"

"Oh, there's no point in going through all that again," interrupted Crysteel. "We'll never get anyone to believe us."

"Hey!" said the stranger, sitting up once more. "What language is that you're speaking? I know a few, but I've never heard anything like that."

"Oh, all right," Crysteel said to Danstor. "You might as well tell him. There's nothing else to do until that policeman comes back anyway."

At this moment, P.C. Hinks was engaged in earnest conversation with the superintendent of the local mental home, who insisted stoutly that all his patients were present. However, a careful check was promised and he'd call back later.

Wondering if the whole thing was a practical joke, P.C. Hinks put the receiver down and quietly made his way to the cells. The three prisoners seemed to be engaged in friendly conversation, so he tiptoed away again. It would do them all good to have a chance to cool down. He rubbed his eye tenderly as he remembered what a battle it had been to get Mr. Graham into the cell during the small hours of the morning.

That young man was now reasonably sober after the night's celebrations, which he did not in the least regret. (It was, after all, quite an occasion when your degree came through and you found you'd got Honours when you'd barely expected a Pass.) But he began to fear that he was still under the influence as Danstor unfolded his tale and waited, not expecting to be believed.

In these circumstances, thought Graham, the best thing to do was to behave as matter-of-factly as possible until the hallucinations got fed up and went away.

"If you really have a spaceship in the hills," he remarked, "surely you can get in touch with it and ask someone to come and rescue you?"

"We want to handle this ourselves," said Crysteel with dignity. "Besides, you don't know our captain."

They sounded very convincing, thought Graham. The whole story hung together remarkably well. And yet . . .

"It's a bit hard for me to believe that you can build interstellar spaceships, but can't get out of a miserable village police station."

Danstor looked at Crysteel, who shuffled uncomfortably.

"We could get out easily enough," said the anthropologist. "But we don't want to use violent means unless it's absolutely essential. You've no idea of the trouble it causes, and the reports we might have to fill in. Besides, if we do get out, I suppose your Flying Squad would catch us before we got back to the ship."

"Not in Little Milton," grinned Graham. "Especially if we could get across to the 'White Hart' without being stopped. My car is over there."

"Oh," said Danstor, his spirits suddenly reviving. He turned to his companion and a lively discussion followed. Then, very gingerly, he produced a small black cylinder from an inner pocket, handling it with much the same confidence as a nervous spinster holding a loaded gun for the first time. Simultaneously, Crysteel retired with some speed to the far corner of the cell.

49

It was at this precise moment that Graham knew, with a sudden icy certainty, that he was stone-sober and that the story he had been listening to was nothing less than the truth.

There was no fuss or bother, no flurry of electric sparks or coloured rays—but a section of the wall three feet across dissolved quietly and collapsed into a little pyramid of sand. The sunlight came streaming into the cell as, with a great sigh of relief, Danstor put his mysterious weapon away.

"Well, come on," he urged Graham. "We're waiting for you."

There were no signs of pursuit, for P.C. Hinks was still arguing on the phone, and it would be some minutes yet before that bright young man returned to the cells and received the biggest shock of his official career. No one at the "White Hart" was particularly surprised to see Graham again; they all knew where and how he had spent the night, and expressed hope that the local Bench would deal leniently with him when his case came up.

With grave misgivings, Crysteel and Danstor climbed into the back of the incredibly ramshackle Bentley which Graham affectionately addressed as "Rose." But there was nothing wrong with the engine under the rusty bonnet, and soon they were roaring out of Little Milton at fifty miles an hour. It was a striking demonstration of the relativity of speed, for Crysteel and Danstor, who had spent the last few years travelling tranquilly through space at several million miles a second, had never been so scared in their lives. When Crysteel had recovered his breath he pulled out his little portable transmitter and called the ship.

"We're on the way back," he shouted above the roar of the wind. "We've got a fairly intelligent human being with us.

Expect us in—whoops!—I'm sorry—we just went over a bridge—about ten minutes. What was that? No, of course not. We didn't have the slightest trouble. Everything went perfectly smoothly. *Goodbye*."

Graham looked back only once to see how his passengers were faring. The sight was rather unsettling, for their ears and hair (which had not been glued on very firmly) had blown away and their real selves were beginning to emerge. Graham began to suspect with some discomfort, that his new acquaintances also lacked noses. Oh well, one could grow used to anything with practice. He was going to have plenty of that in the years ahead.

The rest, of course, you all know; but for the full story of the first landing on Earth, and of the peculiar circumstances under which Ambassador Graham became humanity's representative to the universe at large, has never before been recounted. We extracted the main details, with a good deal of persuasion, from Crysteel and Danstor themselves, while we were working in the Department of Extraterrestrial affairs.

It was understandable, in view of their success on Earth, that they should have been selected by their superiors to make the first contact with our mysterious and secretive neighbours, the Martians. It is also understandable, in the light of the above evidence, that Crysteel and Danstor were so reluctant to embark on this later mission, and we are not really very surprised that nothing has ever been heard of them since.

Into the Comet

"I don't know why I'm recording this," said George Takeo Pickett slowly into the hovering microphone. "There's no chance that anyone will ever hear it. They say the comet will bring us back to the neighbourhood of Earth in about two million years, when it makes its next turn around the sun. I wonder if mankind will still be in existence then, and whether the comet will put on as good a display for our descendants as it did for us? Maybe they'll launch an expedition, just as we have done, to see what they can find. And they'll find us . . .

"For the ship will still be in perfect condition, even after all those ages. There'll be fuel in the tanks, maybe even plenty of air, for our food will give out first, and we'll starve before we suffocate. But I guess we won't wait for that; it will be quicker to open the air lock and get it all over.

"When I was a kid, I read a book on polar exploration called *Winter Amid the Ice*. Well, that's what we're facing now. There's ice all around us, floating in great porous bergs. *Challenger*'s in the middle of a cluster, orbiting round one another so slowly that you have to wait several minutes before you're certain they've moved. But no expedition to Earth's

52

poles ever faced *our* winter. During most of that two million years, the temperature will be four hundred and fifty below zero. We'll be so far away from the sun that it'll give about as much heat as the stars. And who ever tried to warm his hands by Sirius on a cold winter night?"

That absurd image, coming suddenly into his mind, broke him up completely. He could not speak because of memories of moonlight upon snowfields, of Christmas chimes ringing across a land already fifty million miles away. Suddenly he was weeping like a child, his self-control dissolved by the remembrance of all the familiar, disregarded beauties of the Earth he had forever lost.

And everything had begun so well, in such a blaze of excitement and adventure. He could recall (was it only six months ago?) the very first time he had gone out to look for the comet, soon after eighteen-year-old Jimmy Randall had found it in his home made telescope and sent his famous telegram to Mount Stromlo Observatory. In those early days, it had been only a faint polliwog of mist, moving slowly through the constellation of Eridanus, just south of the Equator. It was still far beyond Mars, sweeping sunward along its immensely elongated orbit. When it had last shone in the skies of Earth, there were no men to see it, and there might be none when it appeared again. The human race was seeing Randall's comet for the first and perhaps the only time.

As it approached the sun, it grew, blasting out plumes and jets, the smallest of which was larger than a hundred Earths. Like a great pennant streaming down some cosmic breeze, the comet's tail was already forty million miles long when it raced past the orbit of Mars. It was then that the astronomers realized that this might be the most spectacular sight ever to appear in the heavens; the display put on by Halley's comet, back in 1986, would be nothing in comparison. And it was then that the administrators of the International Astrophysical Decade decided to send the research ship *Challenger* chasing after it, if she could be fitted out in time; for here was a chance that might not come again in a thousand years.

For weeks on end, in the hours before dawn, the comet sprawled across the sky like a second but far brighter Milky Way. As it approached the sun, and felt again the fires it had not known since the mammoths shook the Earth, it became steadily more active. Gouts of luminous gas erupted from its core, forming great fans which turned like slowly swinging searchlights across the stars. The tail, now a hundred million miles long, divided into intricate bands and streamers which changed their patterns completely in the course of a single night. Always they pointed away from the sun, as if driven starwards by a great wind blowing forever outwards from the heart of the solar system.

When the *Challenger* assignment had been given to him, George Pickett could hardly believe his luck. Nothing like this had happened to any reporter since William Laurence and the atom bomb. The facts that he had a science degree, was unmarried, in good health, weighed less than one hundred and twenty pounds, and had no appendix undoubtedly helped. But there must have been many others equally qualified; well, their envy would soon turn to relief.

Because the skimpy pay load of *Challenger* could not accommodate a mere reporter, Pickett had had to double up in his spare time as executive officer. This meant, in practice, that he had to write up the log, act as captain's secretary, keep track of stores, and balance the accounts. It was very fortunate, he often thought, that one needed only three hours' sleep in every twenty-four, in the weightless world of space.

Keeping his two duties separate had required a great deal of tact. When he was not writing in his closet-sized office, or checking the thousands of items stacked away in stores, he would go on the prowl with his recorder. He had been careful, at one time or another, to interview every one of the twenty scientists and engineers who manned *Challenger*. Not all the recordings had been radioed back to Earth; some had been too technical, some too inarticulate, and others too much the reverse. But at least he had played no favourites and, as far as he knew, had trodden on no toes. Not that it mattered now.

He wondered how Dr. Martens was taking it; the astronomer had been one of his most difficult subjects, yet the one who could give most information. On a sudden impulse, Pickett located the earliest of the Martens tapes, and inserted it in the recorder. He knew that he was trying to escape from the present by retreating into the past, but the only effect of that self-knowledge was to make him hope the experiment would succeed.

He still had vivid memories of that first interview, for the weightless microphone, wavering only slightly in the draught of air from the ventilators, had almost hypnotized him into incoherence. Yet no one would have guessed: his voice had its normal, professional smoothness.

They had been twenty million miles behind the comet, but swiftly overtaking it, when he had trapped Martens in the observatory and thrown that opening question at him.

"Dr. Martens," he began, "just what *is* Randall's comet made of?"

"Quite a mixture," the astronomer had answered, "and it's changing all the time as we move away from the sun. But the tail's mostly ammonia, methane, carbon dioxide, water vapour, cyanogen—"

"Cyanogen? Isn't that a poison gas? What would happen if the Earth ran into it?"

"Not a thing. Though it looks so spectacular, by our normal standards a comet's tail is a pretty good vacuum. A volume as big as Earth contains about as much gas as a matchbox full of air."

"And yet this thin stuff puts on such a wonderful display!"

"So does the equally thin gas in an electric sign, and for the same reason. A comet's tail glows because the sun bombards it with electrically charged particles. It's a cosmic sky-sign; one day, I'm afraid, the advertising people will wake up to this, and find a way of writing slogans across the solar system."

"That's a depressing thought—though I suppose someone will claim it's a triumph of applied science. But let's leave the tail; how soon will we get into the heart of the comet—the nucleus, I believe you call it?"

"Since a stern chase always takes a long time, it will be another two weeks before we enter the nucleus. We'll be plough-ing deeper and deeper into the tail, taking a cross section through the comet as we catch up with it. But though the nucleus is still twenty million miles ahead, we've already learned a good deal about it. For one thing, it's extremely small—less than fifty miles across. And even that's not solid, but probably consists of thousands of smaller bodies, all milling round in a cloud."

"Will we be able to go into the nucleus?"

"We'll know when we get there. Maybe we'll play safe and study it through telescopes from a few thousand miles away. But personally, I'll be disappointed unless we go right inside. Won't you?"

Pickett switched off the recorder. Yes, Martens had been right. He *would* have been disappointed, especially since there had seemed no possible source of danger. Nor was there, as far as the comet was concerned. The danger had come from within.

They had sailed through one after another of the huge but unimaginably tenuous curtains of gas that Randall's comet was still ejecting as it raced away from the sun. Yet even now, though they were approaching the densest regions of the nucleus, they were for all practical purposes in a perfect vacuum. The luminous fog that stretched around *Challenger* for so many millions of miles scarcely dimmed the stars; but directly ahead, where lay the comet's core, was a brilliant patch of hazy light, luring them onwards like a will-o'-the-wisp.

The electrical disturbances now taking place around them with ever-increasing violence had almost completely cut their link with Earth. The ship's main radio transmitter could just get a signal through, but for the last few days they had been reduced to sending "O.K." messages in Morse. When they broke away from the comet and headed for home, normal communication would be resumed; but now they were almost as isolated as explorers had been in the days before radio. It was inconvenient, but that was all. Indeed, Pickett rather welcomed this state of affairs; it gave him more time to get on with his clerical duties. Though *Challenger* was sailing into the heart of a comet, on a course that no captain could have dreamed of before the twentieth century, someone still had to check the provisions and count the stores.

Very slowly and cautiously, her radar probing the whole sphere of space around her, *Challenger* crept into the nucleus of the comet. And there she came to rest—amid the ice.

Back in the nineteen-forties, Fred Whipple, of Harvard, had guessed the truth, but it was hard to believe it even when the evidence was before one's eyes. The comet's relatively tiny core was a loose cluster of icebergs, drifting and turning round

one another as they moved along their orbit. But unlike the
bergs that floated in polar seas, they were not a dazzling white,
nor were they made of water. They were a dirty grey, and
very porous, like partly thawed snow. And they were riddled
with pockets of methane and frozen ammonia, which erupted
from time to time in gigantic gas jets as they absorbed the heat
of the sun. It was a wonderful display, but Pickett had little
time to admire it. Now he had far too much.

He had been doing his routine check of the ship's stores
when he came face to face with disaster—though it was some
time before he realized it. For the supply situation had been
perfectly satisfactory; they had ample stocks for the return to
Earth. He had checked that with his own eyes, and now had
merely to confirm the balances recorded in the pinhead-sized
section of the ship's electronic memory which stored all the
accounts.

When the first crazy figures flashed on the screen, Pickett
assumed that he had pressed the wrong key. He cleared the
totals, and fed the information into the computer once more.

Sixty cases of pressed meat to start with; 17 consumed so far;
quantity left: 99999943.

He tried again, and again, with no better result. Then,
feeling annoyed but not particularly alarmed, he went in search
of Dr. Martens.

He found the astronomer in the Torture Chamber—the tiny
gym, squeezed between the technical stores and the bulkhead
of the main propellant tank. Each member of the crew had to
exercise here for an hour a day, lest his muscles waste away
in this gravityless environment. Martens was wrestling with a
set of powerful springs, an expression of grim determination
on his face. It became much grimmer when Pickett gave his
report.

A few tests on the main input board quickly told them the worst. "The computer's insane," said Martens. "It can't even add or subtract."

"But surely we can fix it!"

Martens shook his head. He had lost all his usual cocky self-confidence; he looked, Pickett told himself, like an inflated rubber doll that had started to leak.

"Not even the builders could do that. It's a solid mass of microcircuits, packed as tightly as the human brain. The memory units are still operating, but the computing section's utterly useless. It just scrambles the figures you feed into it."

"And where does that leave us?" Pickett asked.

"It means that we're all dead," Martens answered flatly. "Without the computer, we're done for. It's impossible to calculate an orbit back to Earth. It would take an army of mathematicians weeks to work it out on paper."

"That's ridiculous! The ship's in perfect condition, we've plenty of food and fuel—and you tell me we're all going to die just because we can't do a few sums."

"A *few* sums!" retorted Martens, with a trace of his old spirit. "A major navigational change, like the one needed to break away from the comet and put us on an orbit to Earth involves about a hundred thousand separate calculations. Even the computer needs several minutes for the job."

Pickett was no mathematician, but he knew enough of astronautics to understand the situation. A ship coasting through space was under the influence of many bodies. The main force controlling it was the gravity of the sun, which kept all the planets firmly chained in their orbits. But the planets themselves also tugged it this way and that, though with much feebler strength. To allow for all these conflicting tugs and pulls—above all, to take advantage of them to reach a desired goal scores of millions of miles away—was a problem of fantastic complexity. He could appreciate Martens' despair; no man could work without the tools of his trade, and no trade needed more elaborate tools than this one.

Even after the Captain's announcement, and that first emergency conference when the entire crew had gathered to discuss the situation, it had taken hours for the facts to sink home. The end was still so many months away that the mind could not grasp it; they were under sentence of death, but there was no hurry about the execution. And the view was still superb. . . .

Beyond the glowing mists that enveloped them—and which would be their celestial monument to the end of time—they could see the great beacon of Jupiter, brighter than all the stars. Some of them might still be alive, if the others were willing to sacrifice themselves, when the ship went past the mightiest of the sun's children. Would the extra weeks of life be worth it, Pickett asked himself, to see with your own eyes the sight that Galileo had first glimpsed through his crude telescope four centuries ago—the satellites of Jupiter, shuttling back and forth like beads upon an invisible wire?

Beads upon a wire. With that thought, an all-but-forgotten childhood memory exploded out of his subconscious. It must have been there for days, struggling upward into the light. Now at last it had forced itself upon his waiting mind.

"No!" he cried aloud. "It's ridiculous! They'll laugh at me!"

So what? said the other half of his mind. You've nothing to lose; if it does no more, it will keep everyone busy while the food and the oxygen dwindle away. Even the faintest hope is better than none at all. . . .

He stopped fidgeting with the recorder; the mood of maudlin self-pity was over. Releasing the elastic webbing that held him to his seat, he set off for the technical stores in search of the materials he needed.

"This," said Dr. Martens three days later, "isn't my idea of a joke." He gave a contemptuous glance at the flimsy structure of wire and wood that Pickett was holding in his hand.

"I guessed you'd say that," Pickett replied, keeping his temper under control. "But please listen to me for a minute. My grandmother was Japanese, and when I was a kid she told me a story that I'd completely forgotten about until this week. I think it may save our lives.

"Sometime after the Second World War, there was a contest between an American with an electric desk calculator and a Japanese using an abacus like this. The abacus won."

"Then it must have been a poor desk machine, or an incompetent operator."

"They used the best in the U.S. Army. But let's stop arguing. Give me a test—say a couple of three-figure numbers to multiply."

"Oh—856 times 437."

Pickett's fingers danced over the beads, sliding them up and down the wires with lightning speed. There were twelve wires in all, so that the abacus could handle numbers up to 999,999,-999,999—or could be divided into separate sections where several independent calculations could be carried out simultaneously.

"374072," said Pickett, after an incredibly brief interval of time. "Now see how long *you* take to do it, with pencil and paper."

There was a much longer delay before Martens, who like most mathematicians was poor at arithmetic, called out "375072." A hasty check soon confirmed that Martens had taken at least three times as long as Pickett to arrive at the wrong answer.

The astronomer's face was a study in mingled chagrin, astonishment, and curiosity.

"Where did you learn that trick?" he asked. "I thought those things could only add and subtract."

"Well—multiplication's only repeated addition, isn't it? All I did was to add 856 seven times in the unit column, three times in the tens column, and four times in the hundreds column. You do the same thing when you use pencil and paper. Of course, there are some short cuts, but if you think *I'm* fast, you should have seen my granduncle. He used to work in a Yokohama bank, and you couldn't see his fingers when he was going at speed. He taught me some of the tricks, but I've forgotten most of them in the last twenty years. I've only been practising for a couple of days, so I'm still pretty slow. All the same, I hope I've convinced you that there's something in my argument."

"You certainly have: I'm quite impressed. Can you divide just as quickly?"

"Very nearly, when you've had enough experience."

Martens picked up the abacus, and started flicking the beads back and forth. Then he sighed.

"Ingenious—but it doesn't really help us. Even if it's ten times as fast as a man with pencil and paper—which it isn't— the computer was a million times faster."

"I've thought of that," answered Pickett, a little impatiently.

(Martens had no guts—he gave up too easily. How did he think astonomers managed a hundred years ago, before there were any computers?)

"This is what I propose—tell me if you can see any flaws in it. . . ."

Carefully and earnestly he detailed his plan. As he did so, Martens slowly relaxed, and presently he gave the first laugh that Pickett had heard aboard *Challenger* for days.

"I want to see the skipper's face," said the astronomer, "when you tell him that we're all going back to the nursery to start playing with beads."

There was scepticism at first, but it vanished swiftly when Pickett gave a few demonstrations. To men who had grown up in a world of electronics, the fact that a simple structure of wire and beads could perform such apparent miracles was a revelation. It was also a challenge, and because their lives depended upon it, they responded eagerly.

As soon as the engineering staff had built enough smoothly operating copies of Pickett's crude prototype, the classes began. It took only a few minutes to explain the basic principles; what required time was practice—hour after hour of it, until the fingers flew automatically across the wires and flicked the beads into the right positions without any need for conscious thought. There were some members of the crew who never acquired both accuracy and speed, even after a week of constant practice: but there were others who quickly outdistanced Pickett himself.

They dreamed counters and columns, and flicked beads in their sleep. As soon as they had passed beyond the elementary stage they were divided into teams, which then competed fiercely against each other, until they had reached still higher standards of proficiency. In the end, there were men aboard *Challenger* who could multiply four-figure numbers on the abacus in fifteen seconds, and keep it up hour after hour.

Such work was purely mechanical; it required skill, but no intelligence. The really difficult job was Martens', and there was little that anyone could do to help him. He had to forget all the machine-based techniques he had taken for granted, and rearrange his calculations so that they could be carried out automatically by men who had no idea of the meaning of the figures they were manipulating. He would feed them the basic data, and then they would follow the programme he had laid down. After a few hours of patient routine work, the answer would emerge from the end of the mathematical production line—provided that no mistakes had been made. And the way to guard against that was to have two independent teams working, cross-checking results at regular intervals.

"What we've done," said Pickett into his recorder, when at last he had time to think of the audience he had never expected to speak to again, "is to build a computer out of human beings instead of electronic circuits. It's a few thousand times slower, can't handle many digits, and gets tired easily—but it's doing the job. Not the whole job of navigating to Earth—that's far too complicated—but the simpler one of giving us an orbit that will bring us back into radio range. Once we've escaped from the electrical interference around us, we can radio our position and the big computers on Earth can tell us what to do next.

"We've already broken away from the comet and are no longer heading out of the solar system. Our new orbit checks with the calculations, to the accuracy that can be expected. We're still inside the comet's tail, but the nucleus is a million miles away and we won't see those ammonia icebergs again. They're racing on towards the stars into the freezing night between the suns, while we are coming home. . . .

"Hello, Earth . . . hello, Earth! This is *Challenger* calling, *Challenger* calling. Signal back as soon as you receive us—we'd like you to check our arithmetic—before we work our fingers to the bone!"

No Morning After

"But this is terrible!" said the Supreme Scientist. "Surely there is *something* we can do!"

"Yes, Your Cognizance, but it will be extremely difficult. The planet is more than five hundred light-years away, and it is very hard to maintain contact. However, we believe we can establish a bridgehead. Unfortunately, that is not the only problem. So far, we have been quite unable to communicate with these beings. Their telepathic powers are exceedingly rudimentary—perhaps even nonexistent. And if we cannot talk to them, there is no way in which we can help."

There was a long mental silence while the Supreme Scientist analysed the situation and arrived, as he always did, at the correct answer.

"Any intelligent race must have *some* telepathic individuals," he mused. "We must send out hundreds of observers, tuned to catch the first hint of stray thought. When you find a single responsive mind, concentrate all your efforts upon it. We *must* get our message through."

"Very good, Your Cognizance. It shall be done."

Across the abyss, across the gulf which light itself took half a thousand years to span, the questing intellects of the planet Thaar sent out their tendrils of thought, searching desperately for a single human being whose mind could perceive their presence. And as luck would have it, they encountered William Cross.

At least, they thought it was luck at the time, though later they were not so sure. In any case, they had little choice. The combination of circumstances that opened Bill's mind to them lasted only for seconds, and was not likely to occur again this side of eternity.

There were three ingredients in the miracle: it is hard to say if one was more important than another. The first was the accident of position. A flask of water, when sunlight falls upon it, can act as a crude lens, concentrating the light into a small area. On an immeasurably larger scale, the dense core of the Earth was converging the waves that came from Thaar. In the ordinary way, the radiations of thought are unaffected by matter—they pass through it as effortlessly as light through glass. But there is rather a lot of matter in a planet, and the whole Earth was acting as a gigantic lens. As it turned, it was carrying Bill through its focus, where the feeble thought impulses from Thaar were concentrated a hundredfold.

Yet millions of other men were equally well placed: they received no message. But they were not rocket engineers: they had not spent years thinking and dreaming of space until it had become part of their very being.

And they were not, as Bill was, blind drunk, teetering on the last knife-edge of consciousness, trying to escape from reality into the world of dreams, where there were no disappointments and setbacks.

Of course, he could see the Army's point of view. "You are paid, Dr. Cross," General Potter had pointed out with unnecessary emphasis, "to design missiles, *not*—ah—spaceships.

What you do in your spare time is your own concern, but I must ask you not to use the facilities of the establishment for your hobby. From now on, all projects for the computing section will have to be cleared by me. That is all."

They couldn't sack him, of course: he was too important. But he was not sure that he wanted to stay. He was not really sure of anything except that the job had back-fired on him, and that Brenda had finally gone off with Johnny Gardner—putting events in their order of importance.

Wavering slightly, Bill cupped his chin in his hands and stared at the whitewashed brick wall on the other side of the table. The only attempt at ornamentation was a calendar from Lockheed and a glossy six-by-eight from Aerojet showing L'il Abner Mark I making a boosted take-off. Bill gazed morosely at a spot midway between the two pictures, and emptied his mind of thought. The barriers went down. . . .

At that moment, the massed intellects of Thaar gave a sound-less cry of triumph, and the wall in front of Bill slowly dissolved into a swirling mist. He appeared to be looking down a tunnel that stretched to infinity. As a matter of fact, he was.

Bill studied the phenomenon with mild interest. It had a certain novelty, but was not up to the standard of previous hallucinations. And when the voice started to speak in his mind, he let it ramble on for some time before he did anything about it. Even when drunk, he had an old-fashioned prejudice against starting conversations with himself.

"Bill," the voice began, "listen carefully. We have had great difficulty in contacting you, and this is extremely important."

Bill doubted this on general principles. *Nothing* was im-portant any more.

"We are speaking to you from a very distant planet," continued the voice in a tone of urgent friendliness. "You are the only human being we have been able to contact, so you *must* understand what we are saying."

Bill felt mildly worried, though in an impersonal sort of way, since it was now rather hard to focus on his own problems. How serious was it, he wondered, when you started to hear voices? Well, it was best not to get excited. You can take it or leave it, Dr. Cross, he told himself. Let's take it until it gets to be a nuisance.

"O.K.," he answered with bored indifference. "Go right ahead and talk to me. I won't mind as long as it's interesting."

There was a pause. Then the voice continued, in a slightly worried fashion.

"We don't quite understand. Our message isn't merely *interesting*. It's vital to your entire race, and you must notify your government immediately."

"I'm waiting," said Bill. "It helps to pass the time."

Five hundred light-years away, the Thaarns conferred hastily among themselves. Something seemed to be wrong, but they could not decide precisely what. There was no doubt that they had established contact, yet this was not the sort of reaction they had expected. Well, they could only proceed and hope for the best.

"Listen, Bill," they continued. "Our scientists have just discovered that your sun is about to explode. It will happen three days from now—seventy-four hours, to be exact. Nothing can stop it. But there's no need to be alarmed. We can save you, if you'll do what we say."

"Go on," said Bill. This hallucination was ingenious.

"We can create what we call a bridge—it's a kind of tunnel through space, like the one you're looking into now. The theory is far too complicated to explain, even to one of your mathematicians."

"Hold on a minute!" protested Bill. "I *am* a mathematician, and a darn good one, even when I'm sober. And I've read all about this kind of thing in the science-fiction magazines. I presume you're talking about some kind of short cut through a higher dimension of space. That's old stuff—pre-Einstein."

A sensation of distinct surprise seeped into Bill's mind.

"We had no idea you were so advanced scientifically," said the Thaarns. "But we haven't time to talk about the theory. All that matters is this—if you were to step into that opening in front of you, you'd find yourself instantly on another planet. It's a short cut, as you said—in this case through the thirty-seventh-dimension."

"And it leads to your world?"

"Oh no—you couldn't live here. But there are plenty of planets like Earth in the universe, and we've found one that will suit you. We'll establish bridgeheads like this all over Earth, so your people will only have to walk through them to be saved. Of course, they'll have to start building up civilization again when they reach their new homes, but it's their only hope. You have to pass on this message, and tell them what to do."

"I can just see them listening to me," said Bill. "Why don't you go and talk to the president?"

"Because yours was the only mind we were able to contact. Others seemed closed to us: we don't understand why."

"I could tell you," said Bill, looking at the nearly empty bottle in front of him. He was certainly getting his money's worth. What a remarkable thing the human mind was! Of course, there was nothing at all original in this dialogue: it was easy to see where the ideas came from. Only last week he'd been reading a story about the end of the world, and all this wishful thinking about bridges and tunnels through space was pretty obvious compensation for anyone who'd spent five years wrestling with recalcitrant rockets.

"If the sun does blow up," Bill asked abruptly—trying to catch his hallucination unawares—"what would happen?"

"Why, your planet would be melted instantly. All the planets, in fact, right out to Jupiter."

Bill had to admit that this was quite a grandiose conception. He let his mind play with the thought, and the more he considered it, the more he liked it.

"My dear hallucination," he remarked pityingly, "if I believed you, d'you know what I'd say?"

"But you *must* believe us!" came the despairing cry across the light-years.

Bill ignored it. He was warming to his theme.

"I'd tell you this. *It would be the best thing that could possibly happen.* Yes, it would save a whole lot of misery. No one would have to worry about the Russians and the atom bomb and the high cost of living. Oh, it would be wonderful! It's just what everybody really wants. Nice of you to come along and tell us, but just you go back home and pull your old bridge after you."

There was consternation on Thaar. The Supreme Scientist's brain, floating like a great mass of coral in its tank of nutrient solution, turned slightly yellow about the edges—something it had not done since the Xantil invasion, five thousand years ago. At least fifteen psychologists had nervous breakdowns and were never the same again. The main computer in the College of Cosmophysics started dividing every number in its memory circuits by zero, and promptly blew all its fuses.

And on Earth, Bill Cross was really hitting his stride.

"Look at *me*," he said, pointing a wavering finger at his chest. "I've spent years trying to make rockets do something

70

useful, and they tell me I'm only allowed to build guided missiles, so that we can all blow each other up. The sun will make a neater job of it, and if you did give us another planet we'd only start the whole damn thing all over again."

He paused sadly, marshalling his morbid thoughts.

"And now Brenda heads out of town without even leaving a note. So you'll pardon my lack of enthusiasm for your Boy Scout act."

He couldn't have said "enthusiasm" aloud, Bill realized. But he could still think it, which was an interesting scientific discovery. As he got drunker and drunker, would his cogitation —whoops, *that* nearly threw him!—finally drop down to words of one syllable?

In a final despairing exertion, the Thaarns sent their thoughts along the tunnel between the stars.

"You can't really mean it, Bill! Are *all* human beings like you?"

Now that was an interesting philosophical question! Bill considered it carefully—or as carefully as he could in view of the warm, rosy glow that was now beginning to envelop him. After all, things might be worse. He could get another job, if only for the pleasure of telling General Porter what he could do with his three stars. And as for Brenda—well, women were like streetcars: there'd always be another along in a minute.

Best of all, there was a second bottle of whisky in the Top Secret file. Oh, frabjous day! He rose unsteadily to his feet and wavered across the room.

For the last time, Thaar spoke to Earth.

"Bill!" it repeated desperately. "Surely all human beings can't be like you!"

Bill turned and looked into the swirling tunnel. Strange— it seemed to be lighted with flecks of starlight, and was really rather pretty. He felt proud of himself: not many people could imagine *that*.

"Like me?" he said. "No, they're not." He smiled smugly across the light-years, as the rising tide of euphoria lifted him out of his despondency. "Come to think of it," he added, "there are a lot of people much worse off than me. Yes, I guess I must be one of the lucky ones, after all."

He blinked in mild surprise, for the tunnel had suddenly collapsed upon itself and the whitewashed wall was there again, exactly as it had always been. Thaar knew when it was beaten.

"So much for *that* hallucination," thought Bill. "I was getting tired of it, anyway. Let's see what the next one's like."

As it happened, there wasn't a next one, for five seconds later he passed out cold, just as he was setting the combination of the file cabinet.

The next two days were rather vague and bloodshot, and he forgot all about the interview.

On the third day something was nagging at the back of his mind: he might have remembered if Brenda hadn't turned up again and kept him busy being forgiving.

And there wasn't a fourth day, of course.

"If I Forget Thee, Oh Earth . . ."

When Marvin was ten years old, his father took him through the long, echoing corridors that led up through Administration and Power, until at last they came to the uppermost levels of all and were among the swiftly growing vegetation of the Farmlands. Marvin liked it here: it was fun watching the great, slender plants creeping with almost visible eagerness towards the sunlight as it filtered down through the plastic domes to meet them. The smell of life was everywhere, awakening inexpressible longings in his heart: no longer was he breathing the dry, cool air of the residential levels, purged of all smells but the faint tang of ozone. He wished he could stay here for a little while, but Father would not let him. They went onwards until they had reached the entrance to the Observatory, which he had never visited: but they did not stop, and Marvin knew with a sense of rising excitement that there could be only one goal left. For the first time in his life, he was going Outside.

There were a dozen of the surface vehicles, with their wide balloon tyres and pressurized cabins, in the great servicing chamber. His father must have been expected, for they were led at once to the little scout car waiting by the huge circular door of the air lock. Tense with expectancy, Marvin settled himself down in the cramped cabin while his father started the motor and checked the controls. The inner door of the lock slid open and then closed behind them: he heard the roar of the great air pumps fade slowly away as the pressure dropped to zero. Then the "Vacuum" sign flashed on, the outer door parted, and before Marvin lay the land which he had never yet entered.

He had seen it in photographs, of course: he had watched it imaged on television screens a hundred times. But now it was lying all around him, burning beneath the fierce sun that crawled so slowly across the jet-black sky. He stared into the west, away from the blinding splendour of the sun—and there were the stars, as he had been told but had never quite believed. He gazed at them for a long time, marvelling that anything could be so bright and yet so tiny. They were intense unscintillating points, and suddenly he remembered a rhyme he had once read in one of his father's books:

> *Twinkle, twinkle, little star,*
> *How I wonder what you are.*

Well, *he* knew what the stars were. Whoever asked that question must have been very stupid. And what did they mean by "twinkle"? You could see at a glance that all the stars shone with the same steady, unwavering light. He abandoned the puzzle and turned his attention to the landscape around him.

They were racing across a level plain at almost a hundred miles an hour, the great balloon tyres sending up little spurts of dust behind them. There was no sign of the Colony: in the few minutes while he had been gazing at the stars, its domes and radio towers had fallen below the horizon. Yet there were other indications of man's presence, for about a mile ahead

Marvin could see the curiously shaped structures clustering round the head of a mine. Now and then a puff of vapour would emerge from a squat smokestack and would instantly disperse.

They were past the mine in a moment: Father was driving with a reckless and exhilarating skill as if—it was a strange thought to come into a child's mind—he were trying to escape from something. In a few minutes they had reached the edge of the plateau on which the Colony had been built. The ground fell sharply away beneath them in a dizzying slope whose lower stretches were lost in shadow. Ahead, as far as the eye could reach, was a jumbled wasteland of craters, mountain ranges, and ravines. The crests of the mountains, catching the low sun, burned like islands of fire in a sea of darkness: and above them the stars still shone as steadfastly as ever.

There could be no way forward—yet there was. Marvin clenched his fists as the car edged over the slope and started the long descent. Then he saw the barely visible track leading down the mountainside, and relaxed a little. Other men, it seemed, had gone this way before.

Night fell with a shocking abruptness as they crossed the shadow line and the sun dropped below the crest of the plateau. The twin searchlights sprang into life, casting blue-white bands on the rocks ahead, so that there was scarcely need to check their speed. For hours they drove through valleys and past the foot of mountains whose peaks seemed to comb the stars, and sometimes they emerged for a moment into the sunlight as they climbed over higher ground.

And now on the right was a wrinkled, dusty plain, and on the left, its ramparts and terraces rising mile after mile into the sky, was a wall of mountains that marched into the distance until its peaks sank from sight below the rim of the world. There was no sign that men had ever explored this land, but once they passed the skeleton of a crashed rocket, and beside it a stone cairn surmounted by a metal cross.

It seemed to Marvin that the mountains stretched on forever: but at last, many hours later, the range ended in a towering, precipitous headland that rose steeply from a cluster of little hills. They drove down into a shallow valley that curved in a great arc towards the far side of the mountains: and as they did so, Marvin slowly realized that something very strange was happening in the land ahead.

The sun was now low behind the hills on the right: the valley before them should be in total darkness. Yet it was awash with a cold white radiance that came spilling over the crags beneath which they were driving. Then, suddenly, they were out in the open plain, and the source of the light lay before them in all its glory.

It was very quiet in the little cabin now that the motors had stopped. The only sound was the faint whisper of the oxygen feed and an occasional metallic crepitation as the outer walls of the vehicle radiated away their heat. For no warmth at all came from the great silver crescent that floated low above the far horizon and flooded all this land with pearly light. It was so brilliant that minutes passed before Marvin could accept its challenge and look steadfastly into its glare, but at last he could discern the outlines of continents, the hazy border of the atmosphere, and the white islands of cloud. And even at this distance, he could see the glitter of sunlight on the polar ice.

It was beautiful, and it called to his heart across the abyss of space. There in that shining crescent were all the wonders that he had never known—the hues of sunset skies, the moaning of the sea on pebbled shores, the patter of falling rain, the unhurried benison of snow. These and a thousand others should have been his rightful heritage, but he knew them only from the books and ancient records, and the thought filled him with the anguish of exile.

Why could they not return? It seemed so peaceful beneath those lines of marching cloud. Then Marvin, his eyes no longer blinded by the glare, saw that the portion of the disc that should have been in darkness was gleaming faintly with an evil phosphorescence: and he remembered. He was looking upon the funeral pyre of a world—upon the radioactive aftermath of Armageddon. Across a quarter of a million miles of space, the glow of dying atoms was still visible, a perennial reminder of the ruinous past. It would be centuries yet before that deadly glow died from the rocks and life could return again to fill that silent, empty world.

And now Father began to speak, telling Marvin the story which until this moment had meant no more to him than the fairy tales he had once been told. There were many things he could not understand: it was impossible for him to picture the glowing, multicoloured pattern of life on the planet he had never seen. Nor could he comprehend the forces that had destroyed it in the end, leaving the Colony, preserved by its isolation, as the sole survivor. Yet he could share the agony of those final days, when the Colony had learned at last that never again would the supply ships come flaming down through the stars with gifts from home. One by one the radio stations had ceased to call: on the shadowed globe the lights of the cities had dimmed and died, and they were alone at last, as no men had ever been alone before, carrying in their hands the future of the race.

Then had followed the years of despair, and the long-drawn battle for survival in this fierce and hostile world. That battle had been won, though barely: this little oasis of life was safe against the worst that Nature could do. But unless there was a goal, a future towards which it could work, the Colony would lose the will to live, and neither machines nor skill nor science could save it then.

So, at last, Marvin understood the purpose of this pilgrimage. He would never walk beside the rivers of that lost and legendary world, or listen to the thunder raging above its softly rounded hills. Yet one day—how far ahead?—his children's children would return to claim their heritage. The winds and the rains would scour the poisons from the burning lands and carry them to the sea, and in the depths of the sea they would waste their venom until they could harm no living things. Then the great ships that were still waiting here on the silent, dusty plains could lift once more into space, along the road that led to home.

That was the dream: and one day, Marvin knew with a sudden flash of insight, he would pass it on to his own son, here at this same spot with the mountains behind him and the silver light from the sky streaming into his face.

He did not look back as they began the homeward journey. He could not bear to see the cold glory of the crescent Earth fade from the rocks around him, as he went to rejoin his people in their long exile.

Who's There?

When Satellite Control called me, I was writing up the day's progress report in the Observation Bubble—the glass-domed office that juts out from the axis of the Space Station like the hubcap of a wheel. It was not really a good place to work, for the view was too overwhelming. Only a few yards away I could see the construction teams performing their slow-motion ballet as they put the station together like a giant jigsaw puzzle. And beyond them, twenty thousand miles below, was the blue-green glory of the full Earth, floating against the ravelled star clouds of the Milky Way.

"Station Supervisor here," I answered. "What's the trouble?"

"Our radar's showing a small echo two miles away, almost stationary, about five degrees west of Sirius. Can you give us a visual report on it?"

Anything matching our orbit so precisely could hardly be a meteor; it would have to be something we'd dropped—perhaps an inadequately secured piece of equipment that had drifted away from the station. So I assumed; but when I pulled out my binoculars and searched the sky around Orion, I soon found my mistake. Though this space traveller was man-made, it had nothing to do with us.

"I've found it," I told Control. "It's someone's test satellite —cone-shaped, four antennae, and what looks like a lens system in its base. Probably U.S. Air Force, early nineteen-sixties, judging by the design. I know they lost track of several when their transmitters failed. There were quite a few attempts to hit this orbit before they finally made it."

After a brief search through the files, Control was able to confirm my guess. It took a little longer to find out that Washington wasn't in the least bit interested in our discovery of a twenty-year-old stray satellite, and would be just as happy if we lost it again.

"Well, we can't do *that*," said Control. "Even if nobody wants it, the thing's a menace to navigation. Someone had better go out and haul it aboard."

That someone, I realized, would have to be me. I dared not detach a man from the closely knit construction teams, for we were already behind schedule—and a single day's delay on this job cost a million dollars. All the radio and TV networks on Earth were waiting impatiently for the moment when they could route their programmes through us, and thus provide the first truly global service, spanning the world from Pole to Pole.

"I'll go out and get it," I answered, snapping an elastic band over my papers so that the air currents from the ventilators wouldn't set them wandering around the room. Though I tried to sound as if I was doing everyone a great favour, I was secretly not at all displeased. It had been at least two weeks since I'd been outside; I was getting a little tired of stores schedules, maintenance reports, and all the glamorous ingredients of a Space Station Supervisor's life.

The only member of the staff I passed on my way to the air

lock was Tommy, our recently acquired cat. Pets mean a great deal to men thousands of miles from Earth, but there are not many animals that can adapt themselves to a weightless environment. Tommy mewed plaintively at me as I clambered into my spacesuit, but I was in too much of a hurry to play with him.

At this point, perhaps I should remind you that the suits we use on the station are completely different from the flexible affairs men wear when they want to walk around on the moon. Ours are really baby spaceships, just big enough to hold one man. They are stubby cylinders, about seven feet long, fitted with low-powered propulsion jets, and have a pair of accordion like sleeves at the upper end for the operator's arms. Normally, however, you keep your hands drawn inside the suit, working the manual controls in front of your chest.

As soon as I'd settled down inside my very exclusive spacecraft, I switched on power and checked the gauges on the tiny instrument panel. There's a magic word, "FORB," that you'll often hear spacemen mutter as they climb into their suits; it reminds them to test fuel, oxygen, radio, batteries. All my needles were well in the safety zone, so I lowered the transparent hemisphere over my head and sealed myself in. For a short trip like this, I did not bother to check the suit's internal lockers, which were used to carry food and special equipment for extended missions.

As the conveyor belt decanted me into the air lock, I felt like an Indian papoose being carried along on its mother's back. Then the pumps brought the pressure down to zero, the outer door opened, and the last traces of air swept me out into the stars, turning very slowly head over heels.

The station was only a dozen feet away, yet I was now an independent planet—a little world of my own. I was sealed up in a tiny, mobile cylinder, with a superb view of the entire universe, but I had practically no freedom of movement inside the suit. The padded seat and safety belts prevented me from turning around, though I could reach all the controls and lockers with my hands or feet.

In space, the great enemy is the sun, which can blast you to blindness in seconds. Very cautiously, I opened up the dark filters on the "night" side of my suit, and turned my head to look out at the stars. At the same time I switched the helmet's external sunshade to automatic, so that whichever way the suit gyrated my eyes would be shielded from that intolerable glare.

Presently, I found my target—a bright fleck of silver whose metallic glint distinguished it clearly from the surrounding stars. I stamped on the jet-control pedal, and felt the mild surge of acceleration as the low-powered rockets set me moving away from the station. After ten seconds of steady thrust, I estimated that my speed was great enough, and cut off the drive. It would take me five minutes to coast the rest of the way, and not much longer to return with my salvage.

And it was at that moment, as I launched myself out into the abyss, that I knew that something was horribly wrong.

It is never completely silent inside a spacesuit; you can always hear the gentle hiss of oxygen, the faint whirr of fans and motors, the susurration of your own breathing—even, if you listen carefully enough, the rhythmic thump that is the pounding of your heart. These sounds reverberate through the suit, unable to escape into the surrounding void; they are the unnoticed background of life in space, for you are aware of them only when they change.

They had changed now; to them had been added a sound which I could not identify. It was an intermittent, muffled thudding, sometimes accompanied by a scraping noise, as of metal upon metal.

I froze instantly, holding my breath and trying to locate the alien sound with my ears. The meters on the control board gave no clues; all the needles were rock-steady on their scales, and there were none of the flickering red lights that would warn of impending disaster. That was some comfort, but not much. I had long ago learned to trust my instincts in such matters; their alarm signals were flashing now, telling me to return to the station before it was too late. . . .

Even now, I do not like to recall those next few minutes, as panic slowly flooded into my mind like a rising tide, overwhelming the dams of reason and logic which every man must erect against the mystery of the universe. I knew then what it was like to face insanity; no other explanation fitted the facts.

For it was no longer possible to pretend that the noise disturbing me was that of some faulty mechanism. Though I was in utter isolation, far from any other human being or indeed any material object, I was not alone. The soundless void was bringing to my ears the faint but unmistakable stirrings of life.

In that first, heart-freezing moment it seemed that something was trying to get into my suit—something invisible, seeking shelter from the cruel and pitiless vacuum of space. I whirled madly in my harness, scanning the entire sphere of vision around me except for the blazing, forbidden cone towards the sun. There was nothing there, of course. There could not be—yet that purposeful scrabbling was clearer than ever.

Despite the nonsense that has been written about us, it is not true that spacemen are superstitious. But can you blame me if, as I came to the end of logic's resources, I suddenly remembered how Bernie Summers had died, no farther from the station than I was at this very moment?

It was one of those "impossible" accidents; it always is.

Three things had gone wrong at once. Bernie's oxygen regulator had run wild and sent the pressure soaring, the safety valve had failed to blow—and a faulty joint had given way instead. In a fraction of a second, his suit was open to space.

I had never known Bernie, but suddenly his fate became of overwhelming importance to me—for a horrible idea had come into my mind. One does not talk about these things, but a damaged spacesuit is too valuable to be thrown away, even if it has killed its wearer. It is repaired, renumbered—and issued to someone else. . . .

What happens to the soul of a man who dies between the stars, far from his native world? Are you still here, Bernie, clinging to the last object that linked you to your lost and distant home?

As I fought the nightmares that were swirling around me—for now it seemed that the scratchings and soft fumblings were coming from all directions—there was one last hope to which I clung. For the sake of my sanity, I had to prove that this wasn't Bernie's suit—that the metal walls so closely wrapped around me had never been another man's coffin.

It took me several tries before I could press the right button and switch my transmitter to the emergency wave-length. "Station!" I gasped. "I'm in trouble! Get records to check my suit history and—"

I never finished; they say my yell wrecked the microphone. But what man alone in the absolute isolation of a spacesuit would *not* have yelled when something patted him softly on the back of the neck?

I must have lunged forward, despite the safety harness, and smashed against the upper edge of the control panel. When the rescue squad reached me a few minutes later, I was still unconscious, with an angry bruise across my forehead.

And so I was the last person in the whole satellite relay

system to know what had happened. When I came to my senses an hour later, all our medical staff was gathered around my bed, but it was quite a while before the doctors bothered to look at me. They were much too busy playing with the three cute little kittens our badly misnamed Tommy had been rearing in the seclusion of my spacesuit's Number Five Storage Locker.

All the Time in the World

When the quiet knock came on the door, Robert Ashton surveyed the room in one swift, automatic movement. Its dull respectability satisfied him and should reassure any visitor. Not that he had any reason to expect the police, but there was no point in taking chances.

"Come in," he said, pausing only to grab Plato's *Dialogues* from the shelf beside him. Perhaps this gesture was a little too ostentatious, but it always impressed his clients.

The door opened slowly. At first, Ashton continued his intent reading, not bothering to glance up. There was the slightest acceleration of his heart, a mild and even exhilarating constriction of the chest. Of course, it couldn't possibly be a flatfoot: someone would have tipped him off. Still, any unheralded visitor was unusual and thus potentially dangerous.

Ashton laid down the book, glanced towards the door and remarked in a noncommittal voice: "What can I do for you?" He did not get up; such courtesies belonged to a past he had buried long ago. Besides, it was a woman. In the circles he now frequented, women were accustomed to receive jewels and clothes and money—but never respect.

Yet there was something about this visitor that drew him slowly to his feet. It was not merely that she was beautiful, but she had a poised and effortless authority that moved her into a different world from the flamboyant doxies he met in the normal course of business. There was a brain and a purpose behind those calm, appraising eyes—a brain, Ashton suspected, the equal of his own.

He did not know how grossly he had underestimated her.

"Mr. Ashton," she began, "let us not waste time. I know who you are and I have work for you. Here are my credentials."

She opened a large, stylish handbag and extracted a thick bundle of notes.

"You may regard this," she said, "as a sample."

Ashton caught the bundle as she tossed it carelessly towards him. It was the largest sum of money he had ever held in his life—at least a hundred fivers, all new and serially numbered. He felt them between his fingers. If they were not genuine, they were so good that the difference was of no practical importance.

He ran his thumb to and fro along the edge of the wad as if feeling a pack for a marked card, and said thoughtfully, "I'd like to know where you got these. If they aren't forgeries, they must be hot and will take some passing."

"They are genuine. A very short time ago they were in the Bank of England. But if they are of no use to you throw them in the fire. I merely let you have them to show that I mean business."

"Go on." He gestured to the only seat and balanced himself on the edge of the table.

She drew a sheaf of papers from the capacious handbag and handed it across to him.

"I am prepared to pay you any sum you wish if you will

secure these items and bring them to me, at a time and place to be arranged. What is more, I will guarantee that you can make the thefts with no personal danger."

Ashton looked at the list, and sighed. The woman was mad. Still, she had better be humoured. There might be more money where this came from.

"I notice," he said mildly, "that all these items are in the British Museum, and that most of them are, quite literally, priceless. By that I mean that you could neither buy nor sell them."

"I do not wish to sell them. I am a collector."

"So it seems. What are you prepared to pay for these acquisitions?"

"Name a figure."

There was a short silence. Ashton weighed the possibilities. He took a certain professional pride in his work, but there were some things that no amount of money could accomplish. Still, it would be amusing to see how high the bidding would go.

He looked at the list again.

"I think a round million would be a very reasonable figure for this lot," he said ironically.

"I fear you are not taking me very seriously. With your contacts, you should be able to dispose of these."

There was a flash of light and something sparkled through the air. Ashton caught the necklace before it hit the ground, and despite himself was unable to suppress a gasp of amazement. A fortune glittered through his fingers. The central diamond was the largest he had ever seen—it must be one of the world's most famous jewels.

His visitor seemed completely indifferent as he slipped the necklace into his pocket. Ashton was badly shaken; he knew she was not acting. To her, that fabulous gem was of no more value than a lump of sugar. This was madness on an unimaginable scale.

"Assuming that you can deliver the money," he said, "how do you imagine that it's physically possible to do what you ask? One might steal a single item from this list, but within a few hours the Museum would be solid with police."

With a fortune already in his pocket, he could afford to be frank. Besides, he was curious to learn more about his fantastic visitor.

She smiled, rather sadly, as if humouring a backward child.

"If I show you the way," she said softly, "will you do it?"

"Yes—for a million."

"Have you noticed anything strange since I came in? Is it not—very quiet?"

Ashton listened. My God, she was right! This room was never completely silent, even at night. There had been a wind blowing over the roof tops; where had it gone now? The distant rumble of traffic had ceased; five minutes ago he had been cursing the engines shunting in the marshalling yard at the end of the road. What had happened to them?

"Go to the window."

He obeyed the order and drew aside the grimy lace curtains with fingers that shook slightly despite all attempt at control. Then he relaxed. The street was quite empty, as it often was at this time in the midmorning. There was no traffic, and hence no reason for sound. Then he glanced down the row of dingy houses towards the shunting yard.

His visitor smiled as he stiffened with the shock.

"Tell me what you see, Mr. Ashton."

He turned slowly, face pale and throat muscles working.

"What are you?" he gasped. "A witch?"

89

"Don't be foolish. There is a simple explanation. It is not the world that has changed—but you."

Ashton stared again at that unbelievable shunting engine, the plume of steam frozen motionless above it as if made from cotton wool. He realized now that the clouds were equally immobile; they should have been scudding across the sky. All around him was the unnatural stillness of the high-speed photograph, the vivid unreality of a scene glimpsed in a flash of lightning.

"You are intelligent enough to realize what is happening, even if you cannot understand how it is done. Your time scale has been altered: a minute in the outer world would be a year in this room."

Again she opened the handbag, and this time brought forth what appeared to be a bracelet of some silvery metal, with a series of dials and switches moulded into it.

"You can call this a personal generator," she said. "With it strapped about your arm, you are invincible. You can come and go without hindrance—you can steal everything on that list and bring it to me before one of the guards in the Museum has blinked an eyelid. When you have finished, you can be miles away before you switch off the field and step back into the normal world.

"Now listen carefully, and do exactly what I say. The field has a radius of about seven feet, so you must keep at least that distance from any other person. Secondly, you must not switch it off again until you have completed your task and I have given you your payment. *This is most important.* Now, the plan I have worked out is this. . . ."

No criminal in the history of the world had ever possessed such power. It was intoxicating—yet Ashton wondered if he

would ever get used to it. He had ceased to worry about explan-
ations, at least until the job was done and he had collected his
reward. Then, perhaps, he would get away from England and
enjoy a well-earned retirement.

His visitor had left a few minutes ahead of him, but when he
stepped out into the street the scene was completely unchanged.
Though he had prepared for it, the sensation was still unnerv-
ing. Ashton felt an impulse to hurry, as if this condition
couldn't possibly last and he had to get the job done before the
gadget ran out of juice. But that, he had been assured, was
impossible.

In the High Street he slowed down to look at the frozen
traffic, the paralysed pedestrians. He was careful, as he had
been warned, not to approach so close to anyone that they came
within his field. How ridiculous people looked when one saw
them like this, robbed of such grace as movement could give,
their mouths half open in foolish grimaces!

Having to seek assistance went against the grain, but some
parts of the job were too big for him to handle by himself.
Besides, he could pay liberally and never notice it. The main
difficulty, Ashton realized, would be to find someone who was
intelligent enough not to be scared—or so stupid that he would
take everything for granted. He decided to try the first possibility.

Tony Marchetti's place was down a side street so close to the
police station that one felt it was really carrying camouflage too
far. As he walked past the entrance, Ashton caught a glimpse of
the duty sergeant at his desk and resisted a temptation to go
inside to combine a little pleasure with business. But that sort
of thing could wait until later.

The door of Tony's opened in his face as he approached.
It was such a natural occurrence in a world where nothing was

normal that it was a moment before Ashton realized its implications. Had his generator failed? He glanced hastily down the street and was reassured by the frozen tableau behind him.

"Well, if it isn't Bob Ashton!" said a familiar voice. "Fancy meeting you as early in the morning as this. That's an odd bracelet you're wearing. I thought I had the only one."

"Hello, Aram," replied Ashton. "It looks as if there's a lot going on that neither of us knows about. Have you signed up Tony, or is he still free?"

"Sorry. We've a little job which will keep him busy for a while."

"Don't tell me. It's at the National Gallery or the Tate."

Aram Albenkian fingered his neat goatee. "Who told you that?" he asked.

"No one. But, after all, you *are* the crookedest art dealer in the trade, and I'm beginning to guess what's going on. Did a tall, very good-looking brunette give you that bracelet and a shopping list?"

"I don't see why I should tell you, but the answer's no. It was a man."

Ashton felt a momentary surprise. Then he shrugged his shoulders. "I might have guessed that there would be more than one of them. I'd like to know who's behind it."

"Have you any theories?" said Albenkian guardedly.

Ashton decided that it would be worth risking some loss of information to test the other's reactions. "It's obvious they're not interested in money—they have all they want and can get more with this gadget. The woman who saw me said she was a collector. I took it as a joke, but I see now that she meant it seriously."

"Why do we come into the picture? What's to stop them doing the whole job themselves?" Albenkian asked.

"Maybe they're frightened. Or perhaps they want our—er—specialized knowledge. Some of the items on my list are rather well cased in. My theory is that they're agents for a mad millionaire."

It didn't hold water, and Ashton knew it. But he wanted to see which leaks Albenkian would try to plug.

"My dear Ashton," said the other impatiently, holding up his wrist. "How do you explain this little thing? I know nothing about science, but even I can tell that it's beyond the wildest dreams of our technologies. There's only one conclusion to be drawn from that."

"Go on."

"These people are from—somewhere else. Our world is being systematically looted of its treasures. You know all this stuff you read about rockets and spaceships? Well, someone else has done it first."

Ashton didn't laugh. The theory was no more fantastic than the facts.

"Whoever they are," he said, "they seem to know their way around pretty well. I wonder how many teams they've got? Perhaps the Louvre and the Prado are being reconnoitred at this very minute. The world is going to have a shock before the day's out."

They parted amicably enough, neither confiding any details of real importance about his business. For a fleeting moment Ashton thought of trying to buy over Tony, but there was no point in antagonizing Albenkian. Steve Regan would have to do. That meant walking about a mile, since of course any form of transport was impossible. He would die of old age before a bus completed the journey. Ashton was not clear what would happen if he attempted to drive a car when the field was operating, and he had been warned not to try any experiments.

It astonished Ashton that even such a nearly certified moron as Steve could take the accelerator so calmly; there was something to be said, after all, for the comic strips which were probably his only reading. After a few words of grossly simplified explanation, Steve buckled on the spare wristlet which, rather to Ashton's surprise, his visitor had handed over without comment. Then they set out on their long walk to the Museum.

Ashton, or his client, had thought of everything. They stopped once at a park bench to rest and enjoy some sandwiches and regain their breath. When at last they reached the Museum, neither felt any the worse for the unaccustomed exercise.

They walked together through the gates of the Museum—unable, despite logic, to avoid speaking in whispers—and up the wide stone steps into the entrance hall. Ashton knew his way perfectly. With whimsical humour he displayed his Reading Room ticket as they walked, at a respectful distance, past the statuesque attendants. It occurred to him that the occupants of the great chamber, for the most part, looked just the same as they normally did, even without the benefit of the accelerator.

It was a straightforward but tedious job collecting the books that had been listed. They had been chosen, it seemed, for their beauty as works of art as much as for their literary content. The selection had been done by someone who knew his job. Had *they* done it themselves, Ashton wondered, or had they bribed other experts as they were bribing him? He wondered if he would ever glimpse the full ramifications of their plot.

There was a considerable amount of panel-smashing to be done, but Ashton was careful not to damage any books, even the unwanted ones. Whenever he had collected enough volumes to make a comfortable load, Steve carried them out into the courtyard and dumped them on the paving stones until a small pyramid had accumulated.

It would not matter if they were left for short periods outside the field of the accelerator. No one would notice their momentary flicker of existence in the normal world.

They were in the library for two hours of their time, and paused for another snack before passing to the next job. On the way Ashton stopped for a little private business. There was a tinkle of glass as the tiny case, standing in solitary splendour, yielded up its treasure: then the manuscript of *Alice* was safely tucked into Ashton's pocket.

Among the antiquities, he was not quite so much at home. There were a few examples to be taken from every gallery, and sometimes it was hard to see the reasons for the choice. It was as if—and again he remembered Albenkian's words—these works of art had been selected by someone with totally alien standards. This time, with a few exceptions, *they* had obviously not been guided by the experts.

For the second time in history the case of the Portland Vase was shattered. In five seconds, thought Ashton, the alarms would be going all over the Museum and the whole building would be in an uproar. And in five seconds he could be miles away. It was an intoxicating thought, and as he worked swiftly to complete his contract he began to regret the price he had asked. Even now, it was not too late.

He felt the quiet satisfaction of the good workman as he watched Steve carry the great silver tray of the Mildenhall Treasure out into the courtyard and place it beside the now impressive pile. "That's the lot," he said. "I'll settle up at my place this evening. Now let's get this gadget off you."

They walked out into High Holborn and chose a secluded side street that had no pedestrians near it. Ashton unfastened the peculiar buckle and stepped back from his cohort, watching him freeze into immobility as he did so. Steve was vulnerable again, moving once more with all other men in the stream of time. But before the alarm had gone out he would have lost himself in the London crowds.

When he re-entered the Museum yard, the treasure had already gone. Standing where it had been was his visitor of—how long ago? She was still poised and graceful, but, Ashton thought, looking a little tired. He approached until their fields merged and they were no longer separated by an impassable gulf of silence. "I hope you're satisfied," he said. "How did you move the stuff so quickly?"

She touched the bracelet around her own wrist and gave a wan smile. "We have many other powers besides this."

"Then why did you need my help?"

"There were technical reasons. It was necessary to remove the objects we required from the presence of other matter. In this way, we could gather only what we needed and not waste our limited—what shall I call them?—transporting facilities. Now may I have the bracelet back?"

Ashton slowly handed over the one he was carrying, but made no effort to unfasten his own. There might be danger in what he was doing, but he intended to retreat at the first sign of it.

"I'm prepared to reduce my fee," he said. "In fact I'll waive all payment—in exchange for this." He touched his wrist, where the intricate metal band gleamed in the sunlight.

She was watching him with an expression as fathomless as the Giaconda smile. (Had *that*, Ashton wondered, gone to join the treasure he had gathered? How much had they taken from the Louvre?)

"I would not call that reducing your fee. All the money in the world could not purchase one of those bracelets."

"Or the things I have given you."

"You are greedy, Mr. Ashton. You know that with an accelerator the entire world would be yours."

"What of that? Do you have any further interest in our planet, now you have taken what you need?"

There was a pause. Then, unexpectedly, she smiled. "So you have guessed I do not belong to your world."

"Yes. And I know that you have other agents besides myself. Do you come from Mars, or won't you tell me?"

"I am quite willing to tell you. But you may not thank me if I do."

Ashton looked at her warily. What did she mean by that? Unconscious of his action, he put his wrist behind his back, protecting the bracelet.

"No, I am not from Mars, or any planet of which you have ever heard. You would not understand *what* I am. Yet I will tell you this. I am from the Future."

"The Future! That's ridiculous!"

"Indeed? I should be interested to know why."

"If that sort of thing were possible, our past history would be full of time travellers. Besides, it would involve a *reductio ad absurdum*. Going into the past could change the present and produce all sorts of paradoxes."

"Those are good points, though not perhaps as original as you suppose. But they only refute the possibility of time travel in general, not in the very special case which concerns us now."

"What is peculiar about it?" he asked.

"On very rare occasions, and by the release of an enormous amount of energy, it is possible to produce a—*singularity*—in time. During the fraction of a second when that singularity occurs, the past becomes accessible to the future, though only in a restricted way. We can send our minds back to you, but not our bodies."

"You mean," said Ashton, "that you are *borrowing* the body I see?"

"Oh, I have paid for it, as I am paying you. The owner has agreed to the terms. We are very conscientious in these matters."

Ashton was thinking swiftly. If this story was true, it gave him a definite advantage.

"You mean," he continued, "that you have no direct control over matter, and must work through human agents?"

"Yes. Even those bracelets were made here, under our mental control."

She was explaining too much too readily, revealing all her weaknesses. A warning signal was flashing in the back of Ashton's mind, but he had committed himself too deeply to retreat.

"Then it seems to me," he said slowly, "that you cannot force me to hand this bracelet back."

"That is perfectly true."

"That's all I want to know."

She was smiling at him now, and there was something in that smile that chilled him to the marrow.

"We are not vindictive or unkind, Mr. Ashton," she said quietly. "What I am going to do now appeals to my sense of justice. You have asked for that bracelet; you can keep it. Now I shall tell you just how useful it will be."

For a moment Ashton had a wild impulse to hand back the accelerator. She must have guessed his thoughts.

"No, it's too late. I insist that you keep it. And I can reassure you on one point. It won't wear out. It will last you"—again that enigmatic smile—"the rest of your life.

"Do you mind if we go for a walk, Mr. Ashton? I have done my work here, and would like to have a last glimpse of your world before I leave it forever."

She turned towards the iron gates, and did not wait for a reply. Consumed by curiosity, Ashton followed.

They walked in silence until they were standing among the frozen traffic of Tottenham Court Road. For a while she stood staring at the busy yet motionless crowds; then she sighed.

"I cannot help feeling sorry for them, and for you. I wonder what you would have made of yourselves."

"What do you mean by that?"

"Just now, Mr. Ashton, you implied that the future cannot reach back into the past, because that would alter history. A shrewd remark, but, I am afraid, irrelevant. You see, *your* world has no more history to alter."

She pointed across the road, and Ashton turned swiftly on his heels. There was nothing there except a newsboy crouching over his pile of papers. A placard formed an impossible curve in the breeze that was blowing through this motionless world. Ashton read the crudely lettered words with difficulty:

SUPER-BOMB TEST TODAY

The voice in his ears seemed to come from a very long way off.

"I told you that time travel, even in this restricted form, requires an enormous release of energy—far more than a single bomb can liberate, Mr. Ashton. But that bomb is only a trigger—"

She pointed to the solid ground beneath their feet. "Do you know anything about your own planet? Probably not; your race has learned so little. But even your scientists have discovered that, two thousand miles down, the Earth has a dense, liquid core. That core is made of compressed matter, and it can exist in either of two stable states. Given a certain stimulus, it can change from one of those states to another, just as a seesaw can

99

tip over at the touch of a finger. But that change, Mr. Ashton, will liberate as much energy as all the earthquakes since the beginning of your world. The oceans and continents will fly into space; the sun will have a second asteroid belt.

"That cataclysm will send its echoes down the ages, and will open up to us a fraction of a second in your time. During that instant, we are trying to save what we can of your world's treasures. It is all that we can do; even if your motives were purely selfish and completely dishonest, you have done your race a service you never intended.

"And now I must return to our ship, where it waits by the ruins of Earth almost a hundred thousand years from now. You can keep the bracelet."

The withdrawal was instantaneous. The woman suddenly froze and became one with the other statues in the silent street. He was alone.

Alone! Ashton held the gleaming bracelet before his eyes, hypnotized by its intricate workmanship and by the powers it concealed. He had made a bargain, and he must keep it. He could live out the full span of his life—at the cost of an isolation no other man had ever known. If he switched off the field, the last seconds of history would tick inexorably away.

Seconds? Indeed, there was less time than that. For he knew that the bomb must already have exploded.

He sat down on the edge of the pavement and began to think. There was no need to panic; he must take things calmly, without hysteria. After all, he had plenty of time.

All the time in the world.

Hide and Seek

We were walking back through the woods when Kingman saw the grey squirrel. Our bag was a small but varied one—three grouse, four rabbits (one, I am sorry to say, an infant in arms) and a couple of pigeons. And contrary to certain dark forecasts, both the dogs were still alive.

The squirrel saw us at the same moment. It knew that it was marked for immediate execution as a result of the damage it had done to the trees on the estate, and perhaps it had lost close relatives to Kingman's gun. In three leaps it had reached the base of the nearest tree, and vanished behind it in a flicker of grey. We saw its face once more, appearing for a moment round the edge of its shield a dozen feet from the ground; but though we waited, with guns levelled hopefully at various branches, we never saw it again.

Kingman was very thoughtful as we walked back across the lawn to the magnificent old house. He said nothing as we handed our victims to the cook—who received them without much enthusiasm—and only emerged from his reverie when we were sitting in the smoking room and he remembered his duties as a host.

"That tree-rat," he said suddenly (he always called them "tree-rats", on the grounds that people were too sentimental to shoot the dear little squirrels), "it reminded me of a very peculiar experience that happened shortly before I retired. Very shortly indeed, in fact."

"I thought it would," said Carson dryly. I gave him a glare: he'd been in the Navy and had heard Kingman's stories before, but they were still new to me.

"Of course," Kingman remarked, slightly nettled, "if you'd rather I didn't . . ."

"Do go on," I said hastily. "You've made me curious. What connection there can possibly be between a grey squirrel and the Second Jovian War I can't imagine."

Kingman seemed mollified.

"I think I'd better change some names," he said thoughtfully, "but I won't alter the places. The story begins about a million kilometres sunward of Mars. . . ."

K.15 was a military intelligence operative. It gave him considerable pain when unimaginative people called him a spy, but at the moment he had much more substantial grounds for complaint. For some days now a fast enemy cruiser had been coming up astern, and though it was flattering to have the undivided attention of such a fine ship and so many highly trained men, it was an honour that K.15 would willingly have forgone.

What made the situation doubly annoying was the fact that his friends would be meeting him off Mars in about twelve hours, aboard a ship quite capable of dealing with a mere cruiser—from which you will gather that K.15 was a person of some importance. Unfortunately, the most optimistic calculation showed that the pursuers would be within accurate gun range in six hours. In some six hours five minutes, therefore, K.15 was likely to occupy an extensive and still expanding volume of space.

There might just be time for him to land on Mars, but that would be one of the worst things he could do. It would certainly annoy the aggressively neutral Martians, and the political complications would be frightful. Moreover, if his friends *had* to come down to the planet to rescue him, it would cost them more than ten kilometres a second in fuel—most of their operational reserve.

He had only one advantage, and that a very dubious one. The commander of the cruiser might guess that he was heading for a rendezvous, but he would not know how close it was or how large was the ship that was coming to meet him. If he could keep alive for only twelve hours, he would be safe. The "if" was a somewhat considerable one.

K.15 looked moodily at his charts, wondering if it was worthwhile to burn the rest of his fuel in a final dash. But a dash to where? He would be completely helpless then, and the pursuing ship might still have enough in her tanks to catch him as he flashed outwards into the empty darkness, beyond all hope of rescue—passing his friends as they came sunward at a relative speed so great that they could do nothing to save him.

With some people, the shorter the expectation of life, the more sluggish are the mental processes. They seem hypnotized by the approach to death, so resigned to their fate that they do nothing to avoid it. K.15, on the other hand, found that his mind worked better in such a desperate emergency. It began to work now as it had seldom done before.

Commander Smith—the name will do as well as any other— of the cruiser *Doradus* was not unduly surprised when K.15 began to decelerate. He had half expected the spy to land on

Mars, on the principle that internment was better than anni-
hilation, but when the plotting room brought the news that
the little scout ship was heading for Phobos, he felt completely
baffled. The inner moon was nothing but a jumble of rock some
twenty kilometres across, and not even the economical Martians
had ever found any use for it. K.15 must be pretty desperate if
he thought it was going to be of any greater value to him.

The tiny scout had almost come to rest when the radar
operator lost it against the mass of Phobos. During the braking
manœuvre, K.15 had squandered most of his lead and the
Doradus was now only minutes away—though she was now
beginning to decelerate lest she overrun him. The cruiser was
scarcely three thousand kilometres from Phobos when she came
to a complete halt: of K.15's ship, there was still no sign. It
should be easily visible in the telescopes, but it was probably
on the far side of the little moon.

It reappeared only a few minutes later, travelling under full
thrust on a course directly away from the sun. It was accelerating
at almost five gravities—and it had broken its radio silence. An
automatic recorder was broadcasting over and over again this
interesting message:

"I have landed on Phobos and am being attacked by a Z-class
cruiser. Think I can hold out until you come, but hurry."

The message wasn't even in code, and it left Commander
Smith a sorely puzzled man. The assumption that K.15 was
still aboard the ship and that the whole thing was a ruse was
just a little too naïve. But it might be a double-bluff: the message
had obviously been left in plain language so that he would
receive it and be duly confused. He could afford neither the
time nor the fuel to chase the scout if K.15 really had landed. It
was clear that reinforcements were on the way, and the sooner
he left the vicinity the better. The phrase "Think I can hold

out until you come" might be a piece of sheer impertinence, or it might mean that help was very near indeed.

Then K.15's ship stopped blasting. It had obviously exhausted its fuel, and was doing a little better than six kilometres a second away from the sun. K.15 *must* have landed, for his ship was now speeding helplessly out of the Solar System. Commander Smith didn't like the message it was broadcasting, and guessed that it was running into the track of an approaching warship at some indefinite distance, but there was nothing to be done about that. The *Doradus* began to move towards Phobos, anxious to waste no time.

On the face of it, Commander Smith seemed the master of the situation. His ship was armed with a dozen heavy guided missiles and two turrets of electromagnetic guns. Against him was one man in a space suit, trapped on a moon only twenty kilometres across. It was not until Commander Smith had his first good look at Phobos, from a distance of less than a hundred kilometres, that he began to realize that, after all, K.15 might have a few cards up his sleeve.

To say that Phobos has a diameter of twenty kilometres, as the astronomy books invariably do, is highly misleading. The word "diameter" implies a degree of symmetry which Phobos most certainly lacks. Like those other lumps of cosmic slag, the asteroids, it is a shapeless mass of rock floating in space with, of course, no hint of an atmosphere and not much more gravity. It turns on its axis once every seven hours thirty-nine minutes, thus keeping the same face always to Mars—which is so close that appreciably less than half the planet is visible, the poles being below the curve of the horizon. Beyond this, there is very little more to be said about Phobos.

K.15 had no time to enjoy the beauty of the crescent world

filling the sky above him. He had thrown all the equipment he could carry out of the air lock, set the controls, and jumped. As the little ship went flaming out towards the stars he watched it go with feelings he did not care to analyse. He had burned his boats with a vengeance, and he could only hope that the oncoming battleship would intercept the radio message as the empty vessel went racing by into nothingness. There was also a faint possibility that the enemy cruiser might go in pursuit, but that was rather too much to hope for.

He turned to examine his new home. The only light was the ochre radiance of Mars, since the sun was below the horizon, but that was quite sufficient for his purpose and he could see very well. He stood in the centre of an irregular plain about two kilometres across, surrounded by low hills over which he could leap rather easily if he wished. There was a story he remembered reading long ago about a man who had accidentally jumped off Phobos: that wasn't quite possible—though it was on Deimos—because the escape velocity was still about ten metres a second. But unless he was careful, he might easily find himself at such a height that it would take hours to fall back to the surface—and that would be fatal. For K.15's plan was a simple one: he must remain as close to the surface of Phobos as possible—*and diametrically opposite the cruiser*. The *Doradus* could then fire all her armament against the twenty kilometres of rock, and he wouldn't even feel the concussion. There were only two serious dangers, and one of these did not worry him greatly.

To the layman, knowing nothing of the finer details of astronautics, the plan would have seemed quite suicidal. The *Doradus* was armed with the latest in ultrascientific weapons: moreover, the twenty kilometres which separated her from her prey represented less than a second's flight at maximum speed.

But Commander Smith knew better, and was already feeling rather unhappy. He realized, only too well, that of all the machines of transport man has ever invented, a cruiser of space is far and away the least manœuvrable. It was a simple fact that K.15 could make half a dozen circuits of his little world while her commander was persuading the *Doradus* to make even one.

There is no need to go into technical details, but those who are still unconvinced might like to consider these elementary facts. A rocket-driven spaceship can, obviously, only accelerate along its major axis—that is, "forward". Any deviation from a straight course demands a physical turning of the ship, so that the motors can blast in another direction. Everyone knows that this is done by internal gyros or tangential steering jets, but very few people know just how long this simple manœuvre takes. The average cruiser, fully fuelled, has a mass of two or three thousand tons, which does not make for rapid footwork. But things are even worse than this, for it isn't the mass, but the moment of inertia that matters here—and since a cruiser is a long, thin object, its moment of inertia is slightly colossal. The sad fact remains (though it is seldom mentioned by astronautical engineers) that it takes a good ten minutes to rotate a spaceship through one hundred and eighty degrees, with gyros of any reasonable size. Control jets aren't much quicker, and in any case their use is restricted because the rotation they produce is permanent and they are liable to leave the ship spinning like a slow-motion pinwheel, to the annoyance of all inside.

In the ordinary way, these disadvantages are not very grave. One has millions of kilometres and hundreds of hours in which to deal with such minor matters as a change in the ship's orientation. It is definitely against the rules to move in ten-kilometre-radius circles, and the commander of the *Doradus* felt distinctly aggrieved. K.15 wasn't playing fair.

At the same moment that resourceful individual was taking stock of the situation, which might very well have been worse. He had reached the hills in three jumps and felt less naked than he had out in the open plain. The food and equipment he had taken from the ship he had hidden where he hoped he could find it again, but since his suit could keep him alive for over a day that was the least of his worries. The small packet that was the cause of all the trouble was still with him, in one of those numerous hiding places a well-designed space suit affords.

There was an exhilarating loneliness about his mountain eyrie, even though he was not quite as lonely as he would have wished. Forever fixed in his sky, Mars was waning almost visibly as Phobos swept above the night side of the planet. He could just make out the lights of some of the Martian cities, gleaming pin points marking the junctions of the invisible canals. All else was stars and silence and a line of jagged peaks so close it seemed he could almost touch them. Of the *Doradus* there was still no sign. She was presumably carrying out a careful telescopic examination of the sunlighted side of Phobos.

Mars was a very useful clock: when it was half full the sun would rise and, very probably, so would the *Doradus*. But she might approach from some quite unexpected quarter: she might even—and this was the one real danger—she might even have landed a search party.

This was the first possibility that had occurred to Commander Smith when he saw just what he was up against. Then he realized that the surface area of Phobos was over a thousand square kilometres and that he could not spare more than ten men from his crew to make a search of that jumbled wilderness. Also, K.15 would certainly be armed.

Considering the weapons which the *Doradus* carried, this last objection might seem singularly pointless. It was very far from being so. In the ordinary course of business, side arms and other portable weapons are as much use to a space-cruiser as are cutlasses and crossbows. The *Doradus* happened, quite by chance—and against regulations at that—to carry one automatic pistol and a hundred rounds of ammunition. Any search party would therefore consist of a group of unarmed men looking for a well-concealed and very desperate individual who could pick them off at his leisure. K.15 was breaking the rules again.

The terminator of Mars was now a perfectly straight line, and at almost the same moment the sun came up, not so much like thunder as like a salvo of atomic bombs. K.15 adjusted the filters of his visor and decided to move. It was safer to stay out of the sunlight, not only because here he was less likely to be detected in the shadow but also because his eyes would be much more sensitive there. He had only a pair of binoculars to help him, whereas the *Doradus* would carry an electronic telescope of twenty-centimetres aperture at least.

It would be best, K.15 decided, to locate the cruiser if he could. It might be a rash thing to do, but he would feel much happier when he knew exactly where she was and could watch her movements. He could then keep just below the horizon, and the glare of the rockets would give him ample warning of any impending move. Cautiously launching himself along an almost horizontal trajectory, he began the circumnavigation of his world.

The narrowing crescent of Mars sank below the horizon until only one vast horn reared itself enigmatically against the stars. K.15 began to feel worried: there was still no sign of the *Doradus*. But this was hardly surprising, for she was painted black as night and might be a good hundred kilometres away in space. He stopped, wondering if he had done the right thing after all. Then he noticed that something quite large was eclipsing the stars almost vertically overhead, and was moving swiftly even as he watched. His heart stopped for a moment: then he was himself again, analysing the situation and trying to discover how he had made so disastrous a mistake.

It was some time before he realized that the black shadow slipping across the sky was not the cruiser at all, but something almost equally deadly. It was far smaller, and far nearer, than he had at first thought. The *Doradus* had sent her television-homing guided missiles to look for him.

This was the second danger he had feared, and there was nothing he could do about it except to remain as inconspicuous as possible. The *Doradus* now had many eyes searching for him, but these auxiliaries had very severe limitations. They had been built to look for sunlit spaceships against a background of stars, not to search for a man hiding in a dark jungle of rock. The definition of their television systems was low, and they could only see in that forward direction.

There were rather more men on the chessboard now, and the game was a little deadlier, but his was still the advantage.

The torpedo vanished into the night sky. As it was travelling on a nearly straight course in this low-gravitational field, it would soon be leaving Phobos behind, and K.15 waited for what he knew must happen. A few minutes later, he saw a brief stabbing of rocket exhausts and guessed that the projectile was swinging slowly back on its course. At almost the same moment he saw another flare far away in the opposite quarter of the sky, and wondered just how many of these infernal machines were in action. From what he knew of Z-class cruisers —which was a good deal more than he should—there were four missile-control channels, and they were probably all in use.

He was suddenly struck by an idea so brilliant that he was quite sure it couldn't possibly work. The radio on his suit was a tunable one, covering an unusually wide band, and somewhere not far away the *Doradus* was pumping out power on everything from a thousand megacycles upwards. He switched on the receiver and began to explore.

It came in quickly—the raucous whine of a pulse transmitter not far away. He was probably only picking up a sub-harmonic, but that was quite good enough. It D/F'd sharply, and for the first time K.15 allowed himself to make long-range plans about the future. The *Doradus* had betrayed herself: as long as she operated her missiles, he would know exactly where she was.

He moved cautiously forward towards the transmitter. To his surprise the signal faded, then increased sharply again. This puzzled him until he realized that he must be moving through a diffraction zone. Its width might have told him something useful if he had been a good-enough physicist, but he couldn't imagine what.

The *Doradus* was hanging about five kilometres above the surface, in full sunlight. Her "nonreflecting" paint was overdue for renewal, and K.15 could see her clearly. Since he was still in darkness, and the shadow line was moving away from him, he decided that he was as safe here as anywhere. He settled down comfortably so that he could just see the cruiser and waited, feeling fairly certain that none of the guided projectiles would come so near the ship. By now, he calculated, the commander of the *Doradus* must be getting pretty mad. He was perfectly correct.

After an hour, the cruiser began to heave herself round with all the grace of a bogged hippopotamus. K.15 guessed what was happening. Commander Smith was going to have a look at the antipodes, and was preparing for the perilous fifty-kilometre journey. He watched very carefully to see the orientation the ship was adopting, and when she came to rest again was relieved to see that she was almost broadside to him. Then, with a series of jerks that could not have been very enjoyable aboard, the cruiser began to move down to the horizon. K.15 followed her at a comfortable walking pace—if one could use the phrase—reflecting that this was a feat very few people had ever performed. He was particularly careful not to overtake her on one of his kilometre-long glides, and kept a close watch for any missiles that might be coming up astern.

It took the *Doradus* nearly an hour to cover the fifty kilometres. This, as K.15 amused himself by calculating, represented considerably less than a thousandth of her normal speed. Once, she found herself going off into space at a tangent, and rather than waste time turning end over end again, fired off a salvo of shells to reduce speed. But she made it at last, and K.15 settled down for another vigil, wedged between two rocks where he could just see the cruiser and he was quite sure she couldn't see him. It ocurred to him that by this time Commander Smith might have grave doubts as to whether he really was on Phobos at all, and he felt like firing off a signal flare to reassure him. However, he resisted the temptation.

There would be little point in describing the events of the next ten hours, since they differed in no important detail from those that had gone before. The *Doradus* made three other moves, and K.15 stalked her with the care of a big-game hunter following the spoor of some elephantine beast. Once, when she would have led him out into full sunlight, he let her fall below the horizon until he could only just pick up her signals. But most of the time he kept her just visible, usually low down behind some convenient hill.

Once, a torpedo exploded some kilometres away, and K.15 guessed that some exasperated operator had seen a shadow he didn't like—or else that a technician had forgotten to switch off a proximity fuse. Otherwise nothing happened to enliven the proceedings: in fact, the whole affair was becoming rather boring. He almost welcomed the sight of an occasional guided missile drifting inquisitively overhead, for he did not believe that they could see him if he remained motionless and in reasonable cover. If he could have stayed on the part of Phobos exactly opposite the cruiser he would have been safe even from these, he realized, since the ship would have no control there in the moon's radio-shadow. But he could think of no reliable way in which he could be sure of staying in the safety zone if the cruiser moved again.

The end came very abruptly. There was a sudden blast of steering jets, and the cruiser's main drive burst forth in all its power and splendour. In seconds the *Doradus* was shrinking sunward, free at last, thankful to leave, even in defeat, this miserable lump of rock that had so annoyingly balked her of her legitimate prey. K.15 knew what had happened, and a great sense of peace and relaxation swept over him. In the radar room of the cruiser, someone had seen an echo of disconcerting amplitude approaching with altogether excessive speed. K.15 now had only to switch on his suit beacon and to wait. He could even afford the luxury of a cigarette.

"Quite an interesting story," I said, "and I see now how it ties up with that squirrel. But it does raise one or two queries in my mind."

"Indeed?" said Rupert Kingman politely.

I always like to get to the bottom of things, and I knew that my host had played a part in the Jovian War about which he very seldom spoke. I decided to risk a long shot in the dark.

"May I ask how you happen to know so much about this unorthodox military engagement? It isn't possible, is it, that *you* were K.15?"

There was an odd sort of strangling noise from Carson. Then Kingman said, quite calmly: "No, I wasn't."

He got to his feet and went off towards the gun room.

"If you'll excuse me a moment, I'm going to have another shot at that tree-rat. Maybe I'll get him this time." Then he was gone.

Carson looked at me as if to say: "This is another house you'll never be invited to again." When our host was out of earshot he remarked in a coldly cynical voice:

"You've done it. What did you have to say that for?"

"Well, it seemed a safe guess. How else could he have known all that?"

"As a matter of fact, I believe he met K.15 after the War: they must have had an interesting conversation together. But I thought you knew that Rupert was retired from the service with only the rank of lieutenant commander. The Court of Inquiry could never see his point of view. After all, it just wasn't reasonable that the commander of the fastest ship in the Fleet couldn't catch a man in a space suit."

Robin Hood, F.R.S.

We had landed early in the dawn of the long lunar day, and the slanting shadows lay all around us, extending for miles across the plain. They would slowly shorten as the sun rose higher in the sky, until at noon they would almost vanish— but noon was still five days away, as we measured time on Earth, and nightfall was seven days later still. We had almost two weeks of daylight ahead of us before the sun set and the bluely gleaming Earth became the mistress of the sky.

There was little time for exploration during those first hectic days. We had to unload the ships, grow accustomed to the alien conditions surrounding us, learn to handle our electrically powered tractors and scooters, and erect the igloos that would serve as homes, offices, and labs until the time came to leave. At a pinch, we could live in the spaceships, but it would be excessively uncomfortable and cramped. The igloos were not exactly commodious, but they were luxury after five days in space. Made of tough, flexible plastic, they were blown up like balloons, and their interiors were then partitioned into separate rooms. Air locks allowed access to the outer world, and a good deal of plumbing linked to the ships' air-purification plants kept the atmosphere breathable. Needless to say, the American igloo was the biggest one, and had come complete with everything, *including* the kitchen sink—not to. mention a washing machine, which we and the Russians were always borrowing.

It was late in the "afternoon"—about ten days after we had landed—before we were properly organized and could think about serious scientific work. The first parties made nervous little forays out into the wilderness around the base, familiarizing themselves with the territory. Of course, we already possessed minutely detailed maps and photographs of the region in which we had landed, but it was surprising how misleading they could sometimes be. What had been marked as a small hill on a chart often looked like a mountain to a man toiling along in a space suit, and apparently smooth plains were often covered knee-deep with dust, which made progress extremely slow and tedious.

These were minor difficulties, however, and the low gravity— which gave all objects only a sixth of their terrestrial weight— compensated for much. As the scientists began to accumulate their results and specimens, the radio and TV circuits with Earth became busier and busier, until they were in continuous operation. We were taking no chances; even if *we* didn't get home, the knowledge we were gathering would do so.

The first of the automatic supply rockets landed two days before sunset, precisely according to plan. We saw its braking jets flame briefly against the stars, then blast again a few seconds before touchdown. The actual landing was hidden from us, since for safety reasons the dropping ground was three miles from the base. And on the moon, three miles is well over the curve of the horizon.

When we got to the robot, it was standing slightly askew on its tripod shock absorbers, but in perfect condition. So was everything aboard it, from instruments to food. We carried the stores back to base in triumph, and had a celebration that was really rather overdue. The men had been working too hard, and could do with some relaxation.

It was quite a party; the highlight, I think, was Commander Krasnin trying to do a Cossack dance in a space suit. Then we turned our minds to competitive sports, but found that, for obvious reasons, outdoor activities were somewhat restricted. Games like croquet or bowls would have been practical had we had the equipment; but cricket and football were definitely out. In that gravity, even a football would go half a mile if it were given a good kick—and a cricket ball would never be seen again.

Professor Trevor Williams was the first person to think of a practical lunar sport. He was our astronomer, and also one of the youngest men ever to be made a Fellow of the Royal Society, being only thirty when this ultimate accolade was conferred upon him. His work on methods of interplanetary navigation had made him world famous; less well known, however, was his skill as a toxophilite. For two years in succession he had been archery champion for Wales. I was not surprised, therefore, when I discovered him shooting at a target propped up on a pile of lunar slag.

The bow was a curious one, strung with steel control wire and shaped from a laminated plastic bar. I wondered where Trevor had got hold of it, then remembered that the robot freight rocket had now been cannibalized and bits of it were appearing in all sorts of unexpected places. The arrows, however, were the really interesting feature. To give them stability on the airless moon, where, of course, feathers would be useless, Trevor had managed to rifle them. There was a little gadget on the bow that set them spinning, like bullets, when they were fired, so that they kept on course when they left the bow.

Even with this rather makeshift equipment, it was possible to shoot a mile if one wished to. However, Trevor didn't want to waste arrows, which were not easy to make; he was more interested in seeing the sort of accuracy he could get. It was uncanny to watch the almost flat trajectory of the arrows: they seemed to be travelling parallel with the ground. If he wasn't careful, someone warned Trevor, his arrows might become lunar satellites and would hit him in the back when they completed their orbit.

The second supply rocket arrived the next day, but this time things didn't go according to plan. It made a perfect touchdown, but unfortunately the radar-controlled automatic pilot made one of those mistakes that such simple-minded machines delight in doing. It spotted the only really unclimbable hill in the neighbourhood, locked its beam on to the summit of it, and settled down there like an eagle descending upon its mountain eyrie.

Our badly needed supplies were five hundred feet above our heads, and in a few hours night would be falling. What was to be done?

About fifteen people made the same suggestion at once, and for the next few minutes there was a great scurrying about as we rounded up all the nylon line on the base. Soon there was more than a thousand yards of it coiled in neat loops at Trevor's feet while we all waited expectantly. He tied one end to his arrow, drew the bow, and aimed it experimentally straight towards the stars. The arrow rose a little more than half the height of the cliff; then the weight of the line pulled it back.

"Sorry," said Trevor. "I just can't make it. And don't forget—we'd have to send up some kind of grapnel as well, if we want the end to stay up there."

There was much gloom for the next few minutes, as we

watched the coils of line fall slowly back from the sky. The situation was really somewhat absurd. In our ships we had enough energy to carry us a quarter of a million miles from the moon—yet we were baffled by a puny little cliff. If we had time, we could probably find a way up to the top from the other side of the hill, but that would mean travelling several miles. It would be dangerous, and might well be impossible, during the few hours of daylight that were left.

Scientists were never baffled for long, and too many ingenious (sometimes over-ingenious) minds were working on the problem for it to remain unresolved. But this time it was a little more difficult, and only three people got the answer simultaneously. Trevor thought it over, then said noncommittally, "Well, it's worth trying."

The preparations took a little while, and we were all watching anxiously as the rays of the sinking sun crept higher and higher up the sheer cliff looming above us. Even if Trevor could get a line and grapnel up there, I thought to myself, it would not be easy making the ascent while encumbered with a space suit. I have no head for heights, and was glad that several mountaineering enthusiasts had already volunteered for the job.

At last everything was ready. The line had been carefully arranged so that it would lift from the ground with the minimum of hindrance. A light grapnel had been attached to the line a few feet behind the arrow; we hoped that it would catch in the rocks up there and wouldn't let us down—all too literally—when we put our trust in it.

This time, however, Trevor was not using a single arrow. He attached four to the line, at two-hundred-yard intervals. And I shall never forget that incongruous spectacle of the space-suited figure, gleaming in the last rays of the setting sun, as it drew its bow against the sky.

The arrow sped towards the stars, and before it had lifted more than fifty feet Trevor was already fitting the second one to his improvised bow. It raced after its predecessor, carrying the other end of the long loop that was now being hoisted into space. Almost at once the third followed, lifting its section of line—and I swear that the fourth arrow, with its section, was on the way before the first had noticeably slackened its momentum.

Now that there was no question of a single arrow lifting the entire length of line, it was not hard to reach the required altitude. The first two times the grapnel fell back; then it caught firmly somewhere up on the hidden plateau—and the first volunteer began to haul himself up the line. It was true that he weighed only about thirty pounds in this low gravity, but it was still a long way to fall.

He didn't. The stores in the freight rocket started coming down the cliff within the next hour, and everything essential had been lowered before nightfall. I must confess, however, that my satisfaction was considerably abated when one of the engineers proudly showed me the mouth organ he had had sent from Earth. Even then I felt certain that we would all be very tired of that instrument before the long lunar night had ended. . . .

But that, of course, was hardly Trevor's fault. As we walked back to the ship together, through the great pools of shadow that were flowing swiftly over the plain, he made a proposal that, I am sure, has puzzled thousands of people ever since the detailed maps of the first lunar expedition were published.

After all, it does seem a little odd that a flat and lifeless plain, broken by a single small mountain, should now be labelled on all the charts of the moon as Sherwood Forest.

The Fires Within

"This," said Karn smugly, "will interest you. Just take a look at it!"

He pushed across the file he had been reading, and for the *nth* time I decided to ask for his transfer or, failing that, my own.

"What's it about?" I said wearily.

"It's a long report from a Dr. Matthews to the Minister of Science." He waved it in front of me. "Just read it!"

Without much enthusiasm, I began to go through the file. A few minutes later I looked up and admitted grudgingly: "Maybe you're right—this time." I didn't speak again until I'd finished. . . .

My dear Minister (the letter began). As you requested, here is my special report on Professor Hancock's experiments, which have had such unexpected and extraordinary results. I have not had time to cast it into a more orthodox form, but am sending you the dictation just as it stands.

Since you have many matters engaging your attention, perhaps I should briefly summarize our dealings with Professor Hancock. Until 1955, the Professor held the Kelvin Chair of

Electrical Engineering at Brendon University, from which he was granted indefinite leave of absence to carry out his researches. In these he was joined by the late Dr. Clayton, sometime Chief Geologist to the Ministry of Fuel and Power. Their joint research was financed by grants from the Paul Fund and the Royal Society.

The Professor hoped to develop sonar as a means of precise geological surveying. Sonar, as you will know, is the acoustic equivalent of radar, and although less familiar is older by some millions of years, since bats use it very effectively to detect insects and obstacles at night. Professor Hancock intended to send high-powered supersonic pulses into the ground and to build up from the returning echoes an image of what lay beneath. The picture would be displayed on a cathode ray tube and the whole system would be exactly analogous to the type of radar used in aircraft to show the ground through cloud.

In 1957 the two scientists had achieved partial success but had exhausted their funds. Early in 1958 they applied directly to the government for a block grant. Dr. Clayton pointed out the immense value of a device which would enable us to take a kind of X-ray photo of the Earth's crust, and the Minister of Fuel gave it his approval before passing on the application to us. At that time the report of the Bernal Committee had just been published and we were very anxious that deserving cases should be dealt with quickly to avoid further criticisms. I went to see the Professor at once and submitted a favourable report; the first payment of our grant (S/543A/68) was made a few days later. From that time I have been continually in touch with the research and have assisted to some extent with technical advice.

The equipment used in the experiments is complex, but its principles are simple. Very short but extremely powerful pulses of supersonic waves are generated by a special transmitter which revolves continuously in a pool of a heavy organic liquid. The beam produced passes into the ground and "scans" like a radar beam searching for echoes. By a very ingenious time-delay circuit which I will resist the temptation to describe, echoes from any depth can be selected and so pictures of the strata under investigation can be built up on a cathode ray screen in the normal way.

When I first met Professor Hancock his apparatus was rather primitive, but he was able to show me the distribution of rock down to a depth of several hundred feet and we could see quite clearly a part of the Bakerloo Line which passed very near his laboratory. Much of the Professor's success was due to the great intensity of his supersonic bursts; almost from the beginning he was able to generate peak powers of several hundred kilowatts, nearly all of which was radiated into the ground. It was unsafe to remain near the transmitter, and I noticed that the soil became quite warm around it. I was rather surprised to see large numbers of birds in the vicinity, but soon discovered that they were attracted by the hundreds of dead worms lying on the ground.

At the time of Dr. Clayton's death in 1960, the equipment was working at a power level of over a megawatt and quite good pictures of strata a mile down could be obtained. Dr. Clayton had correlated the results with known geographical surveys, and had proved beyond doubt the value of the information obtained.

Dr. Clayton's death in a motor accident was a great tragedy. He had always exerted a stabilizing influence on the Professor, who had never been much interested in the practical applications of his work. Soon afterwards I noticed a distinct change in the Professor's outlook, and a few months later he confided his new ambitions to me. I had been trying to persuade him to publish his results (he had already spent over £50,000 and the Public Accounts Committee was being difficult again), but he asked for a little more time. I think I can best explain his attitude by his own words, which I remember very vividly, for they were expressed with peculiar emphasis.

"Have you ever wondered," he said, "what the Earth really is like inside? We've only scratched the surface with our mines and wells. What lies beneath is as unknown as the other side of the Moon.

"We know that the Earth is unnaturally dense—far denser than the rocks and soil of its crust would indicate. The core may be solid metal, but until now there's been no way of telling. Even ten miles down the pressure must be thirty tons or more to the square inch and the temperature several hundred degrees. What it's like at the centre staggers the imagination: the pressure must be thousands of tons to the square inch. It's strange to think that in two or three years we may have reached the Moon, but when we've got to the stars we'll still be no nearer that inferno four thousand miles beneath our feet.

"I can now get recognizable echoes from two miles down, but I hope to step up the transmitter to ten megawatts in a few months. With that power, I believe the range will be increased to ten miles; and I don't mean to stop there."

I was impressed, but at the same time I felt a little sceptical.

"That's all very well," I said, "but surely the deeper you go the less there'll be to see. The pressure will make any cavities impossible, and after a few miles there will simply be a homogeneous mass getting denser and denser."

"Quite likely," agreed the Professor. "But I can still learn a lot from the transmission characteristics. Anyway, we'll see when we get there!"

That was four months ago; and yesterday I saw the result of

that research. When I answered his invitation the Professor was clearly excited, but he gave me no hint of what, if anything, he had discovered. He showed me his improved equipment and raised the new receiver from its bath. The sensitivity of the pickups had been greatly improved, and this alone had effectively doubled the range, altogether apart from the increased transmitter power. It was strange to watch the steel framework slowly turning and to realize that it was exploring regions, which, in spite of their nearness, man might never reach.

When we entered the hut containing the display equipment, the Professor was strangely silent. He switched on the transmitter, and even though it was a hundred yards away I could feel an uncomfortable tingling. Then the cathode ray tube lit up and the slowly revolving time-base drew the picture I had seen so often before. Now, however, the definition was much improved owing to the increased power and sensitivity of the equipment. I adjusted the depth control and focused on the Underground, which was clearly visible as a dark lane across the faintly luminous screen. While I was watching, it suddenly seemed to fill with mist and I knew that a train was going through.

Presently I continued the descent. Although I had watched this picture many times before, it was always uncanny to see great luminous masses floating towards me and to know that they were buried rocks—perhaps the debris from the glaciers of fifty thousand years ago. Dr. Clayton had worked out a chart so that we could identify the various strata as they were passed, and presently I saw that I was through the alluvial soil and entering the great clay saucer which traps and holds the city's artesian water. Soon that too was passed, and I was dropping down through the bedrock almost a mile below the surface.

The picture was still clear and bright, though there was little to see, for there were now few changes in the ground structure. The pressure was already rising to a thousand atmospheres; soon it would be impossible for any cavity to remain open, for the rock itself would begin to flow. Mile after mile I sank, but only a pale mist floated on the screen, broken sometimes when echoes were returned from pockets or lodes of denser material. They became fewer and fewer as the depth increased—or else they were now so small that they could no longer be seen.

The scale of the picture was, of course, continually expanding. It was now many miles from side to side, and I felt like an airman looking down upon an unbroken cloud ceiling from an enormous height. For a moment a sense of vertigo seized me as I thought of the abyss into which I was gazing. I do not think that the world will ever seem quite solid to me again.

At a depth of nearly ten miles I stopped and looked at the Professor. There had been no alteration for some time, and I knew that the rock must now be compressed into a featureless, homogeneous mass. I did a quick mental calculation and shuddered as I realized that the pressure must be at least thirty tons to the square inch. The scanner was revolving very slowly now, for the feeble echoes were taking many seconds to struggle back from the depths.

"Well, Professor," I said, "I congratulate you. It's a wonderful achievement. But we seem to have reached the core now. I don't suppose there'll be any change from here to the centre."

He smiled a little wryly. "Go on," he said. "You haven't finished yet."

There was something in his voice that puzzled and alarmed me. I looked at him intently for a moment; his features were just visible in the blue-green glow of the cathode ray tube.

"How far down can this thing go?" I asked, as the interminable descent started again.

"Fifteen miles," he said shortly. I wondered how he knew, for the last feature I had seen at all clearly was only eight miles down. But I continued the long fall through the rock, the scanner turning more and more slowly now, until it took almost five minutes to make a complete revolution. Behind me I could hear the Professor breathing heavily, and once the back of my chair gave a crack as his fingers gripped it.

Then, suddenly, very faint markings began to reappear on the screen. I leaned forward eagerly, wondering if this was the first glimpse of the world's iron core. With agonizing slowness the scanner turned through a right angle, then another. And then——

I leaped suddenly out of my chair, cried "My God!" and turned to face the Professor. Only once before in my life had I received such an intellectual shock—fifteen years ago, when I had accidentally turned on the radio and heard of the fall of the first atomic bomb. That had been unexpected, but this was inconceivable. For on the screen had appeared a grid of faint lines, crossing and recrossing to form a perfectly symmetrical lattice.

I know that I said nothing for many minutes, for the scanner made a complete revolution while I stood frozen with surprise. Then the Professor spoke in a soft, unnaturally calm voice.

"I wanted you to see it for yourself before I said anything. That picture is now thirty miles in diameter, and those squares are two or three miles on a side. You'll notice that the vertical lines converge and the horizontal ones are bent into arcs. We're looking at part of an enormous structure of concentric rings; the centre must lie many miles to the north, probably in the region of Cambridge. How much further it extends in the other direction we can only guess."

"But what *is* it, for heaven's sake?"

"Well, it's clearly artificial."

"That's ridiculous! Fifteen miles down!"

The Professor pointed to the screen again. "God knows I've done my best," he said, "but I can't convince myself that Nature could make anything like that."

I had nothing to say, and presently he continued: "I discovered it three days ago, when I was trying to find the maximum range of the equipment. I can go deeper than this, and I rather think that the structure we can see is so dense that it won't transmit my radiations any further.

"I've tried a dozen theories, but in the end I keep returning to one. We know that the pressure down there must be eight or nine thousand atmospheres, and the temperature must be high enough to melt rock. But normal matter is still almost empty space. Suppose that there is life down there—not organic life, of course, but life based on partially condensed matter, matter in which the electron shells are few or altogether missing. Do you see what I mean? To such creatures, even the rock fifteen miles down would offer no more resistance than water— and we and all our world would be as tenuous as ghosts."

"Then that thing we can see——"

"Is a city, or it's equivalent. You've seen its size, so you can judge for yourself the civilization that must have built it. All the world we know—our oceans and continents and mountains —is nothing more than a film of mist surrounding something beyond our comprehension."

Neither of us said anything for a while. I remember feeling a foolish surprise at being one of the first men in the world to learn the appalling truth; for somehow I never doubted that it was the truth. And I wondered how the rest of humanity would react when the revelation came.

Presently I broke into the silence. "If you're right," I said, "why have they—whatever they are—never made contact with us?"

The Professor looked at me rather pityingly. "We think we're good engineers," he said, "but how could *we* reach *them*? Besides, I'm not at all sure that there haven't been contacts. Think of all the underground creatures and the mythology—trolls and kobolds and the rest. No, it's quite impossible—I take it back. Still, the idea *is* rather suggestive."

All the while the pattern on the screen had never changed: the dim network still glowed there, challenging our sanity. I tried to imagine streets and buildings and the creatures going among them, creatures who could make their way through the incandescent rock as a fish swims through water. It was fantastic . . . and then I remembered the incredibly narrow range of temperatures and pressures under which the human race exists. *We*, not they, were the freaks, for almost all the matter in the universe is at temperatures of thousands or even millions of degrees.

"Well," I said lamely, "what do we do now?"

The Professor leaned forward eagerly. "First we must learn a great deal more, and we must keep this an absolute secret until we are sure of the facts. Can you imagine the panic there would be if this information leaked out? Of course, the truth's inevitable sooner or later, but we may be able to break it slowly.

"You'll realize that the geological surveying side of my work is now utterly unimportant. The first thing we have to do is to build a chain of stations to find the extent of the structure. I visualize them at ten-mile intervals towards the north, but I'd like to build the first one somewhere in South London to see how extensive the thing is. The whole job will have to be kept as secret as the building of the first radar chain in the late thirties.

"At the same time, I'm going to push up my transmitter

power again. I hope to be able to beam the output much more narrowly, and so greatly increase the energy concentration. But this will involve all sorts of mechanical difficulties, and I'll need more assistance."

I promised to do my utmost to get further aid, and the Professor hopes that you will soon be able to visit his laboratory yourself. In the meantime I am attaching a photograph of the vision screen, which although not as clear as the original will, I hope, prove beyond doubt that our observations are not mistaken.

I am well aware that our grant to the Interplanetary Society has brought us dangerously near the total estimate for the year, but surely even the crossing of space is less important than the immediate investigation of this discovery which may have the most profound effects on the philosophy and the future of the whole human race.

I sat back and looked at Karn. There was much in the document I had not understood, but the main outlines were clear enough.

"Yes," I said, "this is it! Where's that photograph?"

He handed it over. The quality was poor, for it had been copied many times before reaching us. But the pattern was unmistakable and I recognized it at once.

"They were good scientists," I said admiringly. "That's Callastheon, all right. So we've found the truth at last, even if it has taken us three hundred years to do it."

"Is that surprising," asked Karn, "when you consider the mountain of stuff we've had to translate and the difficulty of copying it before it evaporates?"

I sat in silence for a while, thinking of the strange race whose relics we were examining. Only once—never again!—had I gone up the great vent our engineers had opened into the Shadow World. It had been a frightening and unforgettable experience. The multiple layers of my pressure suit had made movement very difficult, and despite their insulation I could sense the unbelievable cold that was all around me.

"What a pity it was," I mused, "that our emergence destroyed them so completely. They were a clever race, and we might have learned a lot from them."

"I don't think we can be blamed," said Karn. "We never really believed that anything could exist under those awful conditions of near-vacuum, and almost absolute zero. It couldn't be helped."

I did not agree. "I think it proves that they were the more intelligent race. After all, *they* discovered us first. Everyone laughed at my grandfather when he said that the radiation he'd detected from the Shadow World must be artificial."

Karn ran one of his tentacles over the manuscript.

"We've certainly discovered the cause of that radiation," he said. "Notice the date—it's just a year before your grand-father's discovery. The Professor must have got his grant all right!" He laughed unpleasantly. "It must have given him a shock when he saw us coming up to the surface, right under-neath him."

I scarcely heard his words, for a most uncomfortable feeling had suddenly come over me. I thought of the thousands of miles of rock lying below the great city of Callastheon, growing hotter and denser all the way to the Earth's unknown core. And so I turned to Karn.

"That isn't very funny," I said quietly. "It may be our turn next."

The Forgotten Enemy

The thick furs thudded softly to the ground as Professor Millward jerked himself upright on the narrow bed. This time, he was sure, it had been no dream; the freezing air that rasped against his lungs still seemed to echo with the sound that had come crashing out of the night.

He gathered the furs around his shoulders and listened intently. All was quiet again: from the narrow windows on the western walls long shafts of moonlight played upon the endless rows of books, as they played upon the dead city beneath. The world was utterly still; even in the old days the city would have been silent on such a night, and it was doubly silent now.

With weary resolution Professor Millward shuffled out of bed, and doled a few lumps of coke into the glowing brazier. Then he made his way slowly towards the nearest window, pausing now and then to rest his hand lovingly on the volumes he had guarded all these years.

He shielded his eyes from the brilliant moonlight and peered out into the night. The sky was cloudless: the sound he had heard had not been thunder, whatever it might have been. It had come from the north, and even as he waited it came again.

Distance had softened it, distance and the bulk of the hills that lay beyond London. It did not race across the sky with the wantonness of thunder, but seemed to come from a single point far to the north. It was like no natural sound that he had ever heard, and for a moment he dared to hope again.

Only Man, he was sure, could have made such a sound. Perhaps the dream that had kept him here among these treasures of civilization for more than twenty years would soon be a dream no longer. Men were returning to England, blasting their way through the ice and snow with the weapons that science had given them before the coming of the Dust. It was strange that they should come by land, and from the north, but he thrust aside any thoughts that would quench the newly kindled flame of hope.

Three hundred feet below, the broken sea of snow-covered roofs lay bathed in the bitter moonlight. Miles away the tall stacks of Battersea Power Station glimmered like thin white ghosts against the night sky. Now that the dome of St. Paul's had collapsed beneath the weight of snow, they alone challenged his supremacy.

Professor Millward walked slowly back along the book-shelves, thinking over the plan that had formed in his mind. Twenty years ago he had watched the last helicopters climbing heavily out of Regent's Park, the rotors churning the cease-lessly falling snow. Even then, when the silence had closed around him, he could not bring himself to believe that the North had been abandoned forever. Yet already he had waited a whole generation, among the books to which he had dedicated his life.

In those early days he had sometimes heard, over the radio which was his only contact with the South, of the struggle to colonize the now-temperate lands of the Equator. He did not know the outcome of that far-off battle, fought with desperate skill in the dying jungles and across deserts that had already felt the first touch of snow. Perhaps it had failed; the radio had been silent now for fifteen years or more. Yet if men and machines were indeed returning from the north— of all directions—he might again be able to hear their voices as they spoke to one another and to the lands from which they had come.

Professor Millward left the University building perhaps a dozen times a year, and then only through sheer necessity. Over the past two decades he had collected everything he needed from the shops in the Bloomsbury area, for in the final exodus vast supplies of stocks had been left behind through lack of transport. In many ways, indeed, his life could be called luxurious: no professor of English literature had ever been clothed in such garments as those he had taken from an Oxford Street furrier's.

The sun was blazing from a cloudless sky as he shouldered his pack and unlocked the massive gates. Even ten years ago packs of starving dogs had hunted in this area, and though he had seen none for years he was still cautious and always carried a revolver when he went into the open.

The sunlight was so brilliant that the reflected glare hurt his eyes; but it was almost wholly lacking in heat. Although the belt of cosmic dust through which the Solar System was now passing had made little visible difference to the sun's brightness, it had robbed it of all strength. No one knew whether the world would swim out into the warmth again in ten or a thousand years, and civilization had fled southward in search of lands where the word "summer" was not an empty mockery.

The latest drifts had packed hard and Professor Millward had little difficulty in making the journey to Tottenham Court Road. Sometimes it had taken him hours of floundering through the snow, and one year he had been sealed in his great concrete watchtower for nine months.

He kept away from the houses with their dangerous burdens of snow and their Damoclean icicles, and went north until he came to the shop he was seeking. The words above the shattered windows were still bright: "Jenkins & Sons. Radio and Electrical. Television A Speciality."

Some snow had drifted through a broken section of roofing, but the little upstairs room had not altered since his last visit a dozen years ago. The all-wave radio still stood on the table, and empty tins scattered on the floor spoke mutely of the lonely hours he had spent here before all hope had died. He wondered if he must go through the same ordeal again.

Professor Millward brushed the snow from the copy of *The Amateur Radio Handbook for 1965*, which had taught him what little he knew about wireless. The test-meters and batteries were still lying in their half-remembered places, and to his relief some of the batteries still held their charge. He searched through the stock until he had built up the necessary power supplies, and checked the radio as well as he could. Then he was ready.

It was a pity that he could never send the manufacturers the testimonial they deserved. The faint "hiss" from the speaker brought back memories of the B.B.C., of the nine o'clock news and symphony concerts, of all the things he had taken for granted in a world that was gone like a dream. With scarcely controlled impatience he ran across the wavebands, but everywhere there was nothing save that omnipresent hiss. That was disappointing, but no more: he remembered that the real test would come at night. In the meantime he would forage among the surrounding shops for anything that might be useful.

It was dusk when he returned to the little room. A hundred miles above his head, tenuous and invisible, the Heaviside Layer would be expanding outward towards the stars as the sun went down. So it had done every evening for millions of years, and for half a century only, Man had used it for his own purposes, to reflect around the world his messages of hate or peace, to echo with trivialities or to sound with music once called immortal.

Slowly, with infinite patience, Professor Millward began to traverse the shortwave bands that a generation ago had been a babel of shouting voices and stabbing morse. Even as he listened, the faint hope he had dared to cherish began to fade within him. The city itself was no more silent than the once-crowded oceans of ether. Only the faint crackle of thunderstorms half the world away broke the intolerable stillness. Man had abandoned his latest conquest.

Soon after midnight the batteries faded out. Professor Millward did not have the heart to search for more, but curled up in his furs and fell into a troubled sleep. He got what consolation he could from the thought that if he had not proved his theory, he had not disproved it either.

The heatless sunlight was flooding the lonely white road when he began the homeward journey. He was very tired, for he had slept little and his sleep had been broken by the recurring fantasy of rescue.

The silence was suddenly broken by the distant thunder that came rolling over the white roofs. It came—there could be no doubt now—from beyond the northern hills that had once been London's playground. From the buildings on either side little avalanches of snow went swishing out into the wide street; then the silence returned.

Professor Millward stood motionless, weighing, considering, analysing. The sound had been too long-drawn to be an ordinary explosion—he was dreaming again—it was nothing less than the distant thunder of an atomic bomb, burning and blasting away the snow a million tons at a time. His hopes revived, and the disappointments of the night began to fade.

That momentary pause almost cost him his life. Out of a side-street something huge and white moved suddenly into his field of vision. For a moment his mind refused to accept the reality of what he saw; then the paralysis left him and he fumbled desperately for his futile revolver. Padding towards him across the snow, swinging its head from side to side with a hypnotic, serpentine motion, was a huge polar bear.

He dropped his belongings and ran, floundering over the snow towards the nearest buildings. Providentially the Underground entrance was only fifty feet away. The steel grille was closed, but he remembered breaking the lock many years ago. The temptation to look back was almost intolerable, for he could hear nothing to tell how near his pursuer was. For one frightful moment the iron lattice resisted his numbed fingers. Then it yielded reluctantly and he forced his way through the narrow opening.

Out of his childhood there came a sudden, incongruous memory of an albino ferret he had once seen weaving its body ceaselessly across the wire netting of its cage. There was the same reptile grace in the monstrous shape, almost twice as high as a man, that reared itself in baffled fury against the grille. The metal bowed but did not yield beneath the pressure; then the bear dropped to the ground, grunted softly and padded away. It slashed once or twice at the fallen haversack, scattering a few tins of food into the snow, and vanished as silently as it had come.

A very shaken Professor Millward reached the University three hours later, after moving in short bounds from one refuge to the next. After all these years he was no longer alone in the city. He wondered if there were other visitors, and that same night he knew the answer. Just before dawn he heard, quite distinctly, the cry of a wolf from somewhere in the direction of Hyde Park.

By the end of the week he knew that the animals of the North were on the move. Once he saw a reindeer running southward, pursued by a pack of silent wolves, and sometimes in the night there were sounds of deadly conflict. He was amazed that so much life still existed in the white wilderness between London and the Pole. Now something was driving it southward, and the knowledge brought him a mounting excitement. He did not believe that these fierce survivors would flee from anything save Man.

The strain of waiting was beginning to affect Professor Millward's mind, and for hours he would sit in the cold sunlight, his furs wrapped around him, dreaming of rescue and thinking of the way in which men might be returning to England. Perhaps an expedition had come from North America across the Atlantic ice. It might have been years upon its way. But why had it come so far north? His favourite theory was that the Atlantic ice-packs were not safe enough for heavy traffic further to the south.

One thing, however, he could not explain to his satisfaction. There had been no air reconnaissance; it was hard to believe that the art of flight had been lost so soon.

Sometimes he would walk along the ranks of books, whispering now and then to a well-loved volume. There were books here that he had not dared to open for years, they reminded him so poignantly of the past. But now, as the days grew longer and brighter, he would sometimes take down a volume of poetry and re-read his old favourites. Then he would go to the tall windows and shout the magic words over the rooftops, as if they would break the spell that had gripped the world.

It was warmer now, as if the ghosts of lost summers had returned to haunt the land. For whole days the temperature rose above freezing, while in many places flowers were breaking through the snow. Whatever was approaching from the north was nearer, and several times a day that enigmatic roar would go thundering over the city, sending the snow sliding upon a thousand roofs. There were strange, grinding undertones that Professor Millward found baffling and even ominous. At times it was almost as if he were listening to the clash of mighty armies, and sometimes a mad but dreadful thought came into his mind and would not be dismissed. Often he would wake in the night and imagine he heard the sound of mountains moving to the sea.

So the summer wore away, and as the sound of that distant battle drew steadily nearer Professor Millward was the prey of ever more violently alternating hopes and fears. Although he saw no more wolves or bears—they seemed to have fled southward—he did not risk leaving the safety of his fortress. Every morning he would climb to the highest window of the tower and search the northern horizon with field-glasses. But all he ever saw was the stubborn retreat of the snows above Hampstead, as they fought their bitter rearguard action against the sun.

His vigil ended with the last days of the brief summer. The grinding thunder in the night had been nearer than ever before, but there was still nothing to hint at its real distance from the city. Professor Millward felt no premonition as he climbed to the narrow window and raised his binoculars to the northern sky.

As a watcher from the walls of some threatened fortress might have seen the first sunlight glinting on the spears of an advancing army, so in that moment Professor Millward knew the truth. The air was crystal-clear, and the hills were sharp and brilliant against the cold blue of the sky. They had lost almost all their snow. Once he would have rejoiced at that, but it meant nothing now.

Overnight, the enemy he had forgotten had conquered the last defences and was preparing for the final onslaught. As he saw that deadly glitter along the crest of the doomed hills, Professor Millward understood at last the sound he had heard advancing for so many months. It was little wonder he had dreamed of mountains on the march.

Out of the North, their ancient home, returning in triumph to the lands they had once possessed, the glaciers had come again.

The Reluctant Orchid

Though few people in the "White Hart" will concede that any of Harry Purvis' stories are actually *true*, everyone agrees that some are much more probable than others. And on any scale of probability, the affair of the Reluctant Orchid must rate very low indeed.

I don't remember what ingenious gambit Harry used to launch this narrative: maybe some orchid fancier brought his latest monstrosity into the bar, and that set him off. No matter I do remember the story, and after all that's what counts.

The adventures did not, this time, concern any of Harry's numerous relatives, and he avoided explaining just how he managed to know so many of the sordid details. The hero—if you can call him that—of this hothouse epic was an inoffensive little clerk named Hercules Keating. And if you think *that* is the most unlikely part of the story, just stick round a while.

Hercules is not the sort of name you can carry off lightly at the best of times, and when you are four foot nine and look as if you'd have to take a physical-culture course before you can even become a ninety-seven-pound weakling, it is a positive embarrassment. Perhaps it helped to explain why Hercules had very little social life, and all his real friends grew in pots in a humid conservatory at the bottom of his garden. His needs were simple and he spent very little money on himself; consequently his collection of orchids and cacti was really rather remarkable. Indeed, he had a wide reputation among the fraternity of cactophiles, and often received from remote corners of the globe parcels smelling of mould and tropical jungles.

Hercules had only one living relative, and it would have been hard to find a greater contrast than Aunt Henrietta. She was a massive six-footer, usually wore a rather loud line in Harris tweeds, drove a Jaguar with reckless skill, and chain-smoked cigars. Her parents had set their hearts on a boy, and had never been able to decide whether or not their wish had been granted. Henrietta earned a living, and quite a good one, breeding dogs of various shapes and sizes. She was seldom without a couple of her latest models, and they were not the type of portable canine which ladies like to carry in their handbags. The Keating Kennels specialized in Great Danes, Alsations, and Saint Bernards. . . .

Henrietta, rightly despising men as the weaker sex, had never married. However, for some reason she took an avuncular (yes, that is definitely the right word) interest in Hercules, and called to see him almost every weekend. It was a curious kind of relationship: probably Henrietta found that Hercules bolstered up her feelings of superiority. If he was a good example of the male sex, then they were certainly a pretty sorry lot. Yet, if this was Henrietta's motivation, she was unconscious of it and seemed genuinely fond of her nephew. She was patronizing, but never unkind.

As might be expected, her attentions did not exactly help Hercules' own well-developed inferiority complex. At first he had tolerated his aunt; then he came to dread her regular visits, her booming voice, and her bone-crushing handshake; and at last he grew to hate her. Eventually, indeed, his hate was the dominant emotion in his life, exceeding even his love for his orchids. But he was careful not to show it, realizing that if Aunt Henrietta discovered how he felt about her, she would probably break him in two and throw the pieces to her wolf pack.

There was no way, then, in which Hercules could express his pent-up feelings. He had to be polite to Aunt Henrietta even when he felt like murder. And he often did feel like murder, though he knew that there was nothing he would ever do about it. Until one day . . .

According to the dealer, the orchid came from "somewhere in the Amazon region"—a rather vague postal address. When Hercules first saw it, it was not a very prepossessing sight, even to anyone who loved orchids as much as he did. A shapeless root, about the size of a man's fist—that was all. It was redolent of decay, and there was the faintest hint of a rank, carrion smell. Hercules was not even sure that it was viable, and told the dealer as much. Perhaps that enabled him to purchase it for a trifling sum, and he carried it home without much enthusiasm.

It showed no signs of life for the first month, but that did not worry Hercules. Then, one day, a tiny green shoot appeared and started to creep up to the light. After that, progress was rapid. Soon there was a thick, fleshy stem as big as a man's forearm, and coloured a positively virulent green. Near the top of the stem a series of curious bulges circled the plant: otherwise it was completely featureless. Hercules was now quite excited: he was sure that some entirely new species had swum into his ken.

The rate of growth was now really fantastic: soon the plant was taller than Hercules, not that that was saying a great deal. Moreover, the bulges seemed to be developing, and it looked as if at any moment the orchid would burst into bloom. Hercules waited anxiously, knowing how short-lived some flowers can be, and spent as much time as he possibly could in the hothouse. Despite all his watchfulness, the transformation occurred one night while he was asleep.

In the morning, the orchid was fringed by a series of eight dangling tendrils, almost reaching to the ground. They must have developed inside the plant and emerged with—for the vegetable world—explosive speed. Hercules stared at the phenomenon in amazement, and went very thoughtfully to work.

That evening, as he watered the plant and checked its soil, he noticed a still more peculiar fact. The tendrils were thickening, and they were not completely motionless. They had a slight but unmistakable tendency to vibrate, as if possessing a life of their own. Even Hercules, for all his interest and enthusiasm, found this more than a little disturbing.

A few days later, there was no doubt about it at all. When he approached the orchid, the tendrils swayed towards him in an unpleasantly suggestive fashion. The impression of hunger was so strong that Hercules began to feel very uncomfortable indeed, and something started to nag at the back of his mind. It was quite a while before he could recall what it was: then he said to himself, "Of course! How stupid of me!" and went along to the local library. Here he spent a most interesting half hour rereading a little piece by one H. G. Wells entitled, "The Flowering of the Strange Orchid."

"My goodness!" thought Hercules, when he had finished the tale. As yet there had been no stupefying odour which might overpower the plant's intended victim, but otherwise the characteristics were all too similar. Hercules went home in a very unsettled mood indeed.

He opened the conservatory door and stood looking along the avenue of greenery towards his prize specimen. He judged the length of the tendrils—already he found himself calling them tentacles—with great care and walked to within what appeared a safe distance. The plant certainly had an impression of alertness and menace far more appropriate to the animal than the vegetable kingdom. Hercules remembered the unfortunate history of Doctor Frankenstein, and was not amused.

But, really, this was ridiculous! Such things didn't happen in real life. Well, there was one way to put matters to the test. . . .

Hercules went into the house and came back a few minutes later with a broomstick, to the end of which he had attached a piece of raw meat. Feeling a considerable fool, he advanced towards the orchid as a lion tamer might approach one of his charges at mealtime.

For a moment, nothing happened. Then two of the tendrils developed an agitated twitch. They began to sway back and forth, as if the plant was making up its mind. Abruptly, they whipped out with such speed that they practically vanished from view. They wrapped themselves round the meat, and Hercules felt a powerful tug at the end of his broomstick. Then the meat was gone: the orchid was clutching it, if one may mix metaphors slightly, to its bosom.

"Jumping Jehosophat!" yelled Hercules. It was very seldom indeed that he used such strong language.

The orchid showed no further signs of life for twenty-four hours. It was waiting for the meat to become high, and it was also developing its digestive system. By the next day, a network of what looked like short roots had covered the still-visible chunk of meat. By nightfall, the meat was gone.

The plant had tasted blood.

Hercules' emotions as he watched over his prize were curiously mixed. There were times when it almost gave him nightmares, and he foresaw a whole range of horrid possibilities. The orchid was now extremely strong, and if he got within its clutches he would be done for. But, of course, there was not the slightest danger of that. He had arranged a system of pipes so that it could be watered from a safe distance, and its less orthodox food he simply tossed within range of its tentacles. It was now eating a pound of raw meat a day, and he had an uncomfortable feeling that it could cope with much larger quantities if given the opportunity.

Hercules' natural qualms were, on the whole, outweighed by his feeling of triumph that such a botanical marvel had fallen into his hands. Whenever he chose, he could become the most famous orchid-grower in the world. It was typical of his somewhat restricted viewpoint that it never occurred to him that other people besides orchid fanciers might be interested in his pet.

The creature was now about six feet tall, and apparently still growing—though much more slowly than it had been. All the other plants had been moved from its end of the conservatory, not so much because Hercules feared that it might be cannibalistic as to enable him to tend them without danger. He had stretched a rope across the central aisle so that there was no risk of his accidentally walking within range of those eight dangling arms.

It was obvious that the orchid had a highly developed nervous system, and something very nearly approaching intelligence.

It knew when it was going to be fed, and exhibited unmistakable signs of pleasure. Most fantastic of all—though Hercules was still not sure about this—it seemed capable of producing sounds. There were times, just before a meal, when he fancied he could hear an incredibly high-pitched whistle, skirting the edge of audibility. A newborn bat might have had such a voice: he wondered what purpose it served. Did the orchid somehow lure its prey into its clutches by sound? If so, he did not think the technique would work on him.

While Hercules was making these interesting discoveries, he continued to be fussed over by Aunt Henrietta and assaulted by her hounds, which were never as house-trained as she claimed them to be. She would usually roar up the street on a Sunday afternoon with one dog in the seat beside her and another occupying most of the baggage compartment. Then she would bound up the steps two at a time, nearly deafen Hercules with her greeting, half-paralyse him with her hand-shake, and blow cigar smoke in his face. There had been a time when he was terrified that she would kiss him, but he had long since realized that such effeminate behaviour was foreign to her nature.

Aunt Henrietta looked upon Hercules' orchids with some scorn. Spending one's spare time in a hothouse was, she considered, a very effete recreation. When *she* wanted to let off steam, she went big-game hunting in Kenya. This did nothing to endear her to Hercules, who hated blood sports. But despite his mounting dislike for his overpowering aunt, every Sunday afternoon he dutifully prepared tea for her and they had a tête-à-tête together which, on the surface at least, seemed perfectly friendly. Henrietta never guessed that as he poured the tea Hercules often wished it was poisoned: she was, far down beneath her extensive fortifications, a fundamentally goodhearted person and the knowledge would have upset her deeply.

Hercules did not mention his vegetable octopus to Aunt Henrietta. He had occasionally shown her his most interesting specimens, but this was something he was keeping to himself. Perhaps, even before he had fully formulated his diabolical plan, his subconscious was already preparing the ground. . . .

It was late one Sunday evening, when the roar of the Jaguar had died away into the night and Hercules was restoring his shattered nerves in the conservatory, that the idea first came fully fledged into his mind. He was staring at the orchid, noting how the tendrils were now as thick around as a man's thumb, when a most pleasing fantasy suddenly flashed before his eyes. He pictured Aunt Henrietta struggling helplessly in the grip of the monster, unable to escape from its carnivorous clutches. Why, it would be the perfect crime. The distraught nephew would arrive on the scene too late to be of assistance, and when the police answered his frantic call they would see at a glance that the whole affair was a deplorable accident. True, there would be an inquest, but the coroner's censure would be toned down in view of Hercules' obvious grief. . . .

The more he thought of the idea, the more he liked it. He could see no flaws, as long as the orchid co-operated. That, clearly, would be the greatest problem. He would have to plan a course of training for the creature. It already looked sufficiently diabolical; he must give it a disposition to suit its appearance.

Considering that he had no prior experience in such matters, and that there were no authorities he could consult, Hercules proceeded along very sound and businesslike lines. He would use a fishing rod to dangle pieces of meat just outside the orchid's range, until the creature lashed its tentacles in a frenzy. At such times its high-pitched squeak was clearly audible, and Hercules wondered how it managed to produce the sound. He also wondered what its organs of perception were, but this was yet another mystery that could not be solved without close examination. Perhaps Aunt Henrietta, if all went well, would have a brief opportunity of discovering these interesting facts—though she would probably be too busy to report them for the benefit of posterity.

There was no doubt that the beast was quite powerful enough to deal with its intended victim. It had once wrenched a broomstick out of Hercules' grip, and although that in itself proved very little, the sickening "crack" of the wood a moment later brought a smile of satisfaction to its trainer's thin lips. He began to be much more pleasant and attentive to his aunt. In every respect, indeed, he was the model nephew.

When Hercules considered that his picador tactics had brought the orchid into the right frame of mind, he wondered if he should test it with live bait. This was a problem that worried him for some weeks, during which time he would look speculatively at every dog or cat he passed in the street, but he finally abandoned the idea, for a rather peculiar reason. He was simply too kindhearted to put it into practice. Aunt Henrietta would have to be the first victim.

He starved the orchid for two weeks before he put his plan into action. This was as long as he dared risk—he did not wish to weaken the beast—merely to whet its appetite, that the outcome of the encounter might be more certain. And so, when he had carried the teacups back into the kitchen and was sitting upwind of Aunt Henrietta's cigar, he said casually:"I've got something I'd like to show you, Auntie. I've been keeping it as a surprise. It'll tickle you to death."

That, he thought, was not a completely accurate description, but it gave the general idea.

Auntie took the cigar out of her mouth and looked at Hercules with frank surprise.

"Well!" she boomed. "Wonders will never cease! What *have* you been up to, you rascal?" She slapped him playfully on the back and shot all the air out of his lungs.

"You'll never believe it," gritted Hercules, when he had recovered his breath. "It's in the conservatory."

"Eh?" said Auntie, obviously puzzled.

"Yes—come along and have a look. It's going to create a real sensation."

Auntie gave a snort that might have indicated disbelief, but followed Hercules without further question. The two Alsatians now busily chewing up the carpet looked at her anxiously and half rose to their feet, but she waved them away.

"All right, boys," she ordered gruffly. "I'll be back in a minute." Hercules thought this unlikely.

It was a dark evening, and the lights in the conservatory were off. As they entered, Auntie snorted, "Gad, Hercules—the place smells like a slaughterhouse. Haven't met such a stink since I shot that elephant in Bulawayo and we couldn't find it for a week."

"Sorry, Auntie," apologized Hercules, propelling her forward through the gloom. "It's a new fertilizer I'm using. It produces the most stunning results. Go on—another couple of yards. I want this to be a *real* surprise."

"I hope this isn't a joke," said Auntie suspiciously, as she stomped forward.

"I can promise you it's no joke," replied Hercules, standing with his hand on the light switch. He could just see the looming bulk of the orchid: Auntie was now within ten feet of it. He waited until she was well inside the danger zone, and threw the switch.

There was a frozen moment while the scene was transfixed with light. Then Aunt Henrietta ground to a halt and stood, arms akimbo, in front of the giant orchid. For a moment Hercules was afraid she would retreat before the plant could get into action: then he saw that she was calmly scrutinizing it, unable to make up her mind what the devil it was.

It was a full five seconds before the orchid moved. Then the dangling tentacles flashed into action—but not in the way that Hercules had expected. The plant clutched them tightly, protectively, *around itself*—and at the same time it gave a high-pitched scream of pure terror. In a moment of sickening disillusionment, Hercules realized the awful truth.

His orchid was an utter coward. It might be able to cope with the wild life of the Amazon jungle, but coming suddenly upon Aunt Henrietta had completely broken its nerve.

As for its proposed victim, she stood watching the creature with an astonishment which swiftly changed to another emotion. She spun around on her heels and pointed an accusing finger at her nephew.

"Hercules!" she roared. "The poor thing's scared to death. *Have you been bullying it?*"

Hercules could only stand with his head hanging low in shame and frustration.

"N-no, Auntie," he quavered. "I guess it's naturally nervous."

"Well, I'm used to animals. You should have called me before. You must treat them firmly—but gently. Kindness always works, as long as you show them you're the master. There, there, did-dums—don't be frightened of Auntie—she won't hurt you . . ."

It was, thought Hercules in his blank despair, a revolting sight. With surprising gentleness, Aunt Henrietta fussed over the beast, patting and stroking it until the tentacles relaxed and the shrill, whistling scream died away. After a few minutes of this pandering, it appeared to get over its fright. Hercules finally fled with a muffled sob when one of the tentacles crept forward and began to stroke Henrietta's gnarled fingers. . . .

From that day, he was a broken man. What was worse, he could never escape from the consequences of his intended crime. Henrietta had acquired a new pet, and was liable to call not only at weekends but two or three times in between as well. It was obvious she did not trust Hercules to treat the orchid properly, and still suspected him of bullying it. She would bring tasty tidbits that even her dogs had rejected, but which the orchid accepted with delight. The smell, which had so far been confined to the conservatory, began to creep into the house. . . .

And there, concluded Harry Purvis, as he brought this improbable narrative to a close, the matter rests—to the satisfaction of two, at any rate, of the parties concerned. The orchid is happy, and Aunt Henrietta has something (query, someone?) else to dominate. From time to time the creature has a nervous breakdown when a mouse gets loose in the conservatory, and she rushes to console it.

As for Hercules, there is no chance that he will ever give any more trouble to either of them. He seems to have sunk into a kind of vegetable sloth: indeed, said Harry thoughtfully, every day he becomes more and more like an orchid himself.

The harmless variety, of course. . . .

Encounter at Dawn

It was in the last days of the Empire. The tiny ship was far from home, and almost a hundred light-years from the great parent vessel searching through the loosely packed stars at the rim of the Milky Way. But even here it could not escape from the shadow that lay across civilization: beneath that shadow, pausing ever and again in their work to wonder how their distant homes were faring, the scientists of the Galactic Survey still laboured at their never-ending task.

The ship held only three occupants, but among them they carried knowledge of many sciences, and the experience of half a lifetime in space. After the long interstellar night, the star ahead was warming their spirits as they dropped down towards its fires. A little more golden, a trifle more brilliant than the sun that now seemed a legend of their childhood. They knew from past experience that the chance of locating planets here was more than ninety per cent, and for the moment they forgot all else in the excitement of discovery.

They found the first planet within minutes of coming to rest. It was a giant, of a familiar type, too cold for proto-plasmic life and probably possessing no stable surface. So they turned their search sunward, and presently were rewarded.

It was a world that made their hearts ache for home, a world where everything was hauntingly familiar, yet never quite the same. Two great land masses floated in blue-green seas, capped by ice at both poles. There were some desert regions, but the larger part of the planet was obviously fertile. Even from this distance, the signs of vegetation were unmistakably clear.

They gazed hungrily at the expanding landscape as they fell down into the atmosphere, heading towards noon in the subtropics. The ship plummeted through cloudless skies towards a great river, checked its fall with a surge of soundless power, and came to rest among the long grasses by the water's edge.

No one moved: there was nothing to be done until the automatic instruments had finished their work. Then a bell tinkled softly and the lights on the control board flashed in a pattern of meaningful chaos. Captain Altman rose to his feet with a sigh of relief.

"We're in luck," he said. "We can go outside without protection, if the pathogenic tests are satisfactory. What did you make of the place as we came in, Bertrond?"

"Geologically stable—no active volcanoes, at least. I didn't see any trace of cities, but that proves nothing. If there's a civilization here, it may have passed that stage."

"Or not reached it yet?"

Bertrond shrugged. "Either's just as likely. It may take us some time to find out on a planet this size."

"More time than we've got," said Clindar, glancing at the communications panel that linked them to the mother ship and thence to the Galaxy's threatened heart. For a moment there was a gloomy silence. Then Clindar walked to the control board and pressed a pattern of keys with automatic skill.

With a slight jar, a section of the hull slid aside and the fourth member of the crew stepped out on to the new planet, flexing metal limbs and adjusting servomotors to the unaccustomed gravity. Inside the ship, a television screen glimmered into life, revealing a long vista of waving grasses, some trees in the middle distance, and a glimpse of the great river. Clindar punched a button, and the picture flowed steadily across the screen as the robot turned its head.

"Which way shall we go?" Clindar asked.

"Let's have a look at those trees," Altman replied. "If there's any animal life we'll find it there."

"Look!" cried Bertrond. "A bird!"

Clindar's fingers flew over the keyboard: the picture centred on the tiny speck that had suddenly appeared on the left of the screen, and expanded rapidly as the robot's telephoto lens came into action.

"You're right," he said. "Feathers—beak—well up the evolutionary ladder. This place looks promising. I'll start the camera."

The swaying motion of the picture as the robot walked forward did not distract them: they had grown accustomed to it long ago. But they had never become reconciled to this exploration by proxy when all their impulses cried out to them to leave the ship, to run through the grass and to feel the wind blowing against their faces. Yet it was too great a risk to take, even on a world that seemed as fair as this. There was always a skull hidden behind Nature's most smiling face. Wild beasts, poisonous reptiles, quagmires—death could come to the unwary explorer in a thousand disguises. And worst of all were the invisible enemies, the bacteria and viruses against which the only defence might often be a thousand light-years away.

A robot could laugh at all these dangers and even if, as sometimes happened, it encountered a beast powerful enough to destroy it—well, machines could always be replaced.

They met nothing on the walk across the grasslands. If any small animals were disturbed by the robot's passage, they kept outside its field of vision. Clindar slowed the machine as it approached the trees, and the watchers in the spaceship flinched involuntarily at the branches that appeared to slash across their eyes. The picture dimmed for a moment before the controls readjusted themselves to the weaker illumination; then it came back to normal.

The forest was full of life. It lurked in the undergrowth, clambered among the branches, flew through the air. It fled chattering and gibbering through the trees as the robot advanced. And all the while the automatic cameras were recording the pictures that formed on the screen, gathering material for the biologists to analyse when the ship returned to base.

Clindar breathed a sigh of relief when the trees suddenly thinned. It was exhausting work, keeping the robot from smashing into obstacles as it moved through the forest, but on open ground it could take care of itself. Then the picture trembled as if beneath a hammer blow, there was a grinding metallic thud, and the whole scene swept vertiginously upward as the robot toppled and fell.

"What's that?" cried Altman. "Did you trip?"

"No," said Clindar grimly, his fingers flying over the keyboard. "Something attacked from the rear. I hope . . . ah . . . I've still got control."

He brought the robot to a sitting position and swivelled its head. It did not take long to find the cause of the trouble. Standing a few feet away, and lashing its tail angrily, was a large quadruped with a most ferocious set of teeth. At the moment it was, fairly obviously, trying to decide whether to attack again.

Slowly, the robot rose to its feet, and as it did so the great beast crouched to spring. A smile flitted across Clindar's face: he knew how to deal with this situation. His thumb felt for the seldom-used key labelled "Siren."

The forest echoed with a hideous undulating scream from the robots concealed speaker, and the machine advanced to meet it's adversary, arms flailing in front of it. The startled beast almost fell over backwards in its effort to turn, and in seconds was gone from sight.

"Now I suppose we'll have to wait a couple of hours until everything comes out of hiding again," said Bertrond ruefully.

"I don't know much about animal psychology," interjected Altman, "but is it usual for them to attack something completely unfamiliar?"

"Some will attack anything that moves, but that's unusual. Normally they attack only for food, or if they've already been threatened. What are you driving at? Do you suggest that there are other robots on this planet?"

"Certainly not. But our carnivorous friend may have mistaken our machine for a more edible biped. Don't you think that this opening in the jungle is rather unnatural? It could easily be a path."

"In that case," said Clindar promptly, "we'll follow it and find out. I'm tired of dodging trees, but I hope nothing jumps on us again: it's bad for my nerves."

"You were right, Altman," said Bertrond a little later. "It's certainly a path. But that doesn't mean intelligence. After all, animals—"

He stopped in mid-sentence, and at the same instant Clindar brought the advancing robot to a halt. The path had suddenly opened out into a wide clearing, almost completely occupied by a village of flimsy huts. It was ringed by a wooden palisade, obviously defence against an enemy who at the moment presented no threat. For the gates were wide open, and beyond them the inhabitants were going peacefully about their ways.

For many minutes the three explorers stared in silence at the screen. Then Clindar shivered a little and remarked: "It's uncanny. It might be our own planet, a hundred thousand years ago. I feel as if I've gone back in time."

"There's nothing weird about it," said the practical Altman. "After all, we've discovered nearly a hundred planets with our type of life on them."

"Yes," retorted Clindar. "A hundred in the whole Galaxy! I still think it's strange it had to happen to us."

"Well, it had to happen to *somebody*," said Bertrond philosophically. "Meanwhile, we must work out our contact procedure. If we send the robot into the village it will start a panic."

"That," said Altman, "is a masterly understatement. What we'll have to do is catch a native by himself and prove that we're friendly. Hide the robot, Clindar. Somewhere in the woods where it can watch the village without being spotted. We've a week's practical anthropology ahead of us!"

It was three days before the biological tests showed that it would be safe to leave the ship. Even then Bertrond insisted on going alone—alone, that is, if one ignored the substantial company of the robot. With such an ally he was not afraid of this planet's larger beasts, and his body's natural defences could take care of the micro-organisms. So, at least, the analysers had assured him; and considering the complexity of the problem, they made remarkably few mistakes. . . .

He stayed outside for an hour, enjoying himself cautiously, while his companions watched with envy. It would be another three days before they could be quite certain that it was safe to follow Bertrond's example. Meanwhile, they kept busy enough watching the village through the lenses of the robot, and recording everything they could with the cameras. They had moved the spaceship at night so that it was hidden in the depths of the forest, for they did not wish to be discovered until they were ready.

And all the while the news from home grew worse. Though their remoteness here at the edge of the Universe deadened its impact, it lay heavily on their minds and sometimes overwhelmed them with a sense of futility. At any moment, they knew, the signal for recall might come as the Empire summoned up its last resources in its extremity. But until then they would continue their work as though pure knowledge were the only thing that mattered.

Seven days after landing, they were ready to make the experiment. They knew now what paths the villagers used when going hunting, and Bertrond chose one of the less frequented ways. Then he placed a chair firmly in the middle of the path and settled down to read a book.

It was not, of course, quite as simple as that: Bertrond had taken all imaginable precautions. Hidden in the undergrowth fifty yards away, the robot was watching through its telescopic lenses, and in its hand it held a small but deadly weapon. Controlling it from the spaceship, his fingers poised over the keyboard, Clindar waited to do what might be necessary.

That was the negative side of the plan: the positive side was more obvious. Lying at Bertrond's feet was the carcass of a small, horned animal which he hoped would be an acceptable gift to any hunter passing this way.

Two hours later the radio in his suit harness whispered a

warning. Quite calmly, though the blood was pounding in his veins, Bertrond laid aside his book and looked down the trail. The savage was walking forward confidently enough, swinging a spear in his right hand. He paused for a moment when he saw Bertrond, then advanced more cautiously. He could tell that there was nothing to fear, for the stranger was slightly built and obviously unarmed.

When only twenty feet separated them, Bertrond gave a reassuring smile and rose slowly to his feet. He bent down, picked up the carcass, and carried it forward as an offering. The gesture would have been understood by any creature on any world, and it was understood here. The savage reached forward, took the animal, and threw it effortlessly over his shoulder. For an instant he stared into Bertrond's eyes with a fathomless expression; then he turned and walked back towards the village. Three times he glanced round to see if Bertrond was following, and each time Bertrond smiled and waved reassurance. The whole episode lasted little more than a minute. As the first contact between two races it was completely without drama, though not without dignity.

Bertrond did not move until the other had vanished from sight. Then he relaxed and spoke into his suit microphone.

"That was a pretty good beginning," he said jubilantly. "He wasn't in the least frightened, or even suspicious. I think he'll be back."

"It still seems too good to be true," said Altman's voice in his ear. "I should have thought he'd have been either scared or hostile. Would *you* have accepted a lavish gift from a peculiar stranger with such little fuss?"

Bertrond was slowly walking back to the ship. The robot had now come out of cover and was keeping guard a few paces behind him.

"*I* wouldn't," he replied, "but I belong to a civilized community. Complete savages may react to strangers in many different ways, according to their past experience. Suppose this tribe has never had any enemies. That's quite possible on a large but sparsely populated planet. Then we may expect curiosity, but no fear at all."

"If these people have no enemies," put in Clindar, no longer fully occupied in controlling the robot, "why have they got a stockade round the village?"

"I meant no *human* enemies," replied Bertrond. "If that's true, it simplifies our task immensely."

"Do you think he'll come back?"

"Of course. If he's as human as I think, curiosity and greed will make him return. In a couple of days we'll be bosom friends."

Looked at dispassionately, it became a fantastic routine. Every morning the robot would go hunting under Clindar's direction, until it was now the deadliest killer in the jungle. Then Bertrond would wait until Yaan—which was the nearest they could get to his name—came striding confidently along the path. He came at the same time every day, and he always came alone. They wondered about this: did he wish to keep his great discovery to himself and thus get all the credit for his hunting prowess? If so, it showed unexpected foresight and cunning.

At first Yaan had departed at once with his prize, as if afraid that the donor of such a generous gift might change his mind. Soon, however, as Bertrond had hoped, he could be induced to stay for a while by simple conjuring tricks and a display of brightly coloured fabrics and crystals, in which he took a child-like delight. At last Bertrond was able to engage him in lengthy conversations, all of which were recorded as well as being filmed through the eyes of the hidden robot.

One day the philologists might be able to analyse this material; the best that Bertrond could do was to discover the meanings of a few simple verbs and nouns. This was made more difficult by the fact that Yaan not only used different words for the same thing, but sometimes the same word for different things.

Between these daily interviews, the ship travelled far, surveying the planet from the air and sometimes landing for more detailed examinations. Although several other human settlements were observed, Bertrond made no attempt to get in touch with them, for it was easy to see that they were all at much the same cultural level as Yaan's people.

It was, Bertrond often thought, a particularly bad joke on the part of Fate that one of the Galaxy's very few truly human races should have been discovered at this moment of time. Not long ago this would have been an event of supreme importance; now civilization was too hard-pressed to concern itself with these savage cousins waiting at the dawn of history.

Not until Bertrond was sure he had become part of Yaan's everyday life did he introduce him to the robot. He was showing Yaan the patterns in a kaleidoscope when Clindar brought the machine striding through the grass with its latest victim dangling across one metal arm. For the first time Yaan showed something akin to fear; but he relaxed at Bertrond's soothing words, though he continued to watch the advancing monster. It halted some distance away, and Bertrond walked forward to meet it. As he did so, the robot raised its arms and handed him the dead beast. He took it solemnly and carried it back to Yaan, staggering a little under the unaccustomed load.

Bertrond would have given a great deal to know just what Yaan was thinking as he accepted the gift. Was he trying to decide whether the robot was master or slave? Perhaps such conceptions as this were beyond his grasp: to him the robot might be merely another man, a hunter who was a friend of Bertrond.

Clindar's voice, slightly larger than life, came from the robot's speaker.

"It's astonishing how calmly he accepts us. Won't anything scare him?"

"You will keep judging him by your own standards," replied Bertrond. "Remember, his psychology is completely different, and much simpler. Now that he has confidence in me, anything that I accept won't worry him."

"I wonder if that will be true of all his race?" queried Altman. "It's hardly safe to judge by a single specimen. I want to see what happens when we send the robot into the village."

"Hello!" exclaimed Bertrond. "*That* surprised him. He's never met a person who could speak with two voices before."

"Do you think he'll guess the truth when he meets us?" said Clindar.

"No. The robot will be pure magic to him—but it won't be any more wonderful than fire and lightning and all the other forces he must already take for granted."

"Well, what's the next move?" asked Altman, a little impatiently. "Are you going to bring him to the ship, or will you go into the village first?"

Bertrond hesitated. "I'm anxious not to do too much too quickly. You know the accidents that have happened with strange races when that's been tried. I'll let him think this over, and when we get back tomorrow I'll try to persuade him to take the robot back to the village."

In the hidden ship, Clindar reactivated the robot and started it moving again. Like Altman, he was growing a little impatient of this excessive caution, but on all matters relating to alien life-forms Bertrond was the expert, and they had to obey his orders.

There were times now when he almost wished he were a robot himself, devoid of feelings or emotions, able to watch the fall of a leaf or the death agonies of a world with equal detachment. . . .

The sun was low when Yaan heard the great voice crying from the jungle. He recognized it at once, despite its inhuman volume: it was the voice of his friend, and it was calling him.

In the echoing silence, the life of the village came to a stop. Even the children ceased to play: the only sound was the thin cry of a baby frightened by the sudden silence.

All eyes were upon Yaan as he walked swiftly to his hut and grasped the spear that lay beside the entrance. The stockade would soon be closed against the prowlers of the night, but he did not hesitate as he stepped out into the lengthening shadows. He was passing through the gates when once again that mighty voice summoned him, and now it held a note of urgency that came clearly across all the barriers of language and culture.

The shining giant who spoke with many voices met him a little way from the village and beckoned him to follow. There was no sign of Bertrond. They walked for almost a mile before they saw him in the distance, standing not far from the river's edge and staring out across the dark, slowly moving waters.

He turned as Yaan approached, yet for a moment seemed unaware of his presence. Then he gave a gesture of dismissal to the shining one, who withdrew into the distance.

Yaan waited. He was patient and, though he could never have expressed it in words, contented. When he was with Bertrond he felt the first intimations of that selfless, utterly irrational devotion his race would not fully achieve for many ages.

It was a strange tableau. Here at the river's brink two men were standing. One was dressed in a closely fitting uniform equipped with tiny, intricate mechanisms. The other was wearing the skin of an animal and was carrying a flint-tipped spear. Ten thousand generations lay between them, ten thousand generations and an immeasurable gulf of space. Yet they were both human. As she must do often in Eternity, Nature had repeated one of her basic patterns.

Presently Bertrond began to speak, walking to and fro in short, quick steps as he did, and in his voice there was a trace of madness.

"It's all over, Yaan. I'd hoped that with our knowledge we could have brought you out of barbarism in a dozen generations, but now you will have to fight your way up from the jungle alone, and it may take you a million years to do so. I'm sorry— there's so much we could have done. Even now I wanted to stay here, but Altman and Clindar talk of duty, and I suppose that they are right. There is little enough that we can do, but our world is calling and we must not forsake it.

"I wish you could understand me, Yaan. I wish you knew what I was saying. I'm leaving you these tools: some of them you will discover how to use, though as likely as not in a generation they'll be lost or forgotten. See how this blade cuts: it will be ages before your world can make its like. And guard this well: when you press the button—look! If you use it sparingly, it will give you light for years, though sooner or later it will die. As for these other things—find what use for them you can.

"Here come the first stars, up there in the east. Do you ever look at the stars, Yaan? I wonder how long it will be before you

165

have discovered what they are, and I wonder what will have happened to us by then. Those stars are our homes, Yaan, and we cannot save them. Many have died already, in explosions so vast that I can imagine them no more than you. In a hundred thousand of your years, the light of those funeral pyres will reach your world and set its people wondering. By then, perhaps, your race will be reaching for the stars. I wish I could warn you against the mistakes we made, and which now will cost us all that we have won.

"It is well for your people, Yaan, that your world is here at the frontier of the Universe. You may escape the doom that waits for us. One day, perhaps, your ships will go searching among the stars as we have done, and they may come upon the ruins of our worlds and wonder who we were. But they will never know that we met here by this river when your race was young.

"Here come my friends; they would give me no more time. Good-bye, Yaan—use well the things I have left you. They are your world's greatest treasures."

Something huge, something that glittered in the starlight, was sliding down from the sky. It did not reach the ground, but came to rest a little way above the surface, and in utter silence a rectangle of light opened in its side. The shining giant appeared out of the night and stepped through the golden door. Bertrond followed, pausing for a moment at the threshold to wave back at Yaan. Then the darkness closed behind him.

No more swiftly than smoke drifts upward from a fire, the ship lifted away. When it was so small that Yaan felt he could hold it in his hands, it seemed to blur into a long line of light slanting upward into the stars. From the empty sky a peal of thunder echoed over the sleeping land; and Yaan knew at last that the gods were gone and would never come again.

For a long time he stood by the gently moving waters, and into his soul there came a sense of loss he was never to forget and never to understand. Then, carefully and reverently, he collected together the gifts that Bertrond had left.

Under the stars, the lonely figure walked homeward across a nameless land. Behind him the river flowed softly to the sea, winding through the fertile plains on which, more than a thousand centuries ahead, Yaan's descendants would build the great city they were to call Babylon.

Security Check

It is often said that in our age of assembly lines and mass production there's no room for the individual craftsman, the artist in wood or metal who made so many of the treasures of the past. Like most generalizations, this simply isn't true. He's rarer now, of course, but he's certainly not extinct. He has often had to change his vocation, but in his modest way he still flourishes. Even on the island of Manhattan he may be found, if you know where to look for him. Where rents are low and fire regulations unheard of, his minute, cluttered workshops may be discovered in the basements of apartment houses or in the upper storeys of derelict shops. He may no longer make violins or cuckoo clocks or music boxes, but the skills he uses are the same as they always were, and no two objects he creates are ever identical. He is not contemptuous of mechanization: you will find several electric hand tools under the debris on his bench. He has moved with the times: he will always be around, the universal odd-job man who is never aware of it when he makes an immortal work of art.

Hans Muller's workshop consisted of a large room at the back of a deserted warehouse, no more than a vigorous stone's throw from the Queensborough Bridge. Most of the building had been boarded up awaiting demolition, and sooner or later Hans would have to move. The only entrance was across a weed-covered yard used as a parking place during the day, and much frequented by the local juvenile delinquents at night. They had never given Hans any trouble, for he knew better than to co-operate with the police when they made their periodic inquiries. The police fully appreciated his delicate position and did not press matters, so Hans was on good terms with everybody. Being a peaceable citizen, that suited him very well.

The work on which Hans was now engaged would have deeply puzzled his Bavarian ancestors. Indeed, ten years ago it would have puzzled Hans himself. And it had all started because a bankrupt client had given him a TV set in payment for services rendered. . . .

Hans had accepted the offer reluctantly, not because he was old-fashioned and disapproved of TV, but simply because he couldn't imagine where he could find time to look at the darned thing. Still, he thought, at least I can always sell it for fifty dollars. But before I do that, let's see what the programmes are like. . . .

His hand had gone out to the switch: the screen had filled with moving shapes—and, like millions of men before him, Hans was lost. He entered a world he had not known existed—a world of battling spaceships, of exotic planets and strange races—the world, in fact, of Captain Zipp, Commander of the Space Legion.

Only when the tedious recital of the virtues of Crunche, the Wonder Cereal, had given way to an almost equally tedious boxing match between two muscle-bound characters who seemed to have signed a nonaggression pact, did the magic fade. Hans was a simple man. He had always been fond of fairy tales—and *this* was the modern fairy tale, with trimmings of which the Grimm Brothers had never dreamed. So Hans did not sell his TV set.

It was some weeks before the initial naïve, uncritical enjoyment wore off. The first thing that began to annoy Hans was the furniture and general décor in the world of the future. He was, as has been indicated, an artist—and he refused to believe that in a hundred years taste would have deteriorated as badly as the Crunche sponsors seemed to imagine.

He also thought very little of the weapons that Captain Zipp and his opponents used. It was true that Hans did not pretend to understand the principles upon which the portable proton disintegrator was based, but however it worked, there was certainly no reason why it should be *that* clumsy. The clothes, the spaceship interiors—they just weren't convincing. How did he know? He had always possessed a highly developed sense of the fitness of things, and it could still operate even in this novel field.

We have said that Hans was a simple man. He was also a shrewd one, and he had heard that there was money in TV. So he sat down and began to draw.

Even if the producer of Captain Zipp had not lost patience with his set designer, Hans Muller's ideas would certainly have made him sit up and take notice. There was an authenticity and realism about them that made them quite outstanding. They were completely free from the element of phonyness that had begun to upset even Captain Zipp's most juvenile followers. Hans was hired on the spot.

He made his own conditions, however. What he was doing he did largely for love, notwithstanding the fact that it was earning him more money than anything he had ever done before in his life. He would take no assistants, and would remain in his little workshop. All that he wanted to do was to produce the prototypes, the basic designs. The mass production could be done somewhere else—he was a craftsman, not a factory.

The arrangement had worked well. Over the last six months Captain Zipp had been transformed and was now the despair of all the rival space operas. This, his viewers thought, was not just a serial about the future. It *was* the future—there was no argument about it. Even the actors seemed to have been inspired by their new surroundings: off the set, they sometimes behaved like twentieth-century time travellers stranded in the Victorian Age, indignant because they no longer had access to the gadgets that had always been part of their lives.

But Hans knew nothing about this. He toiled away happily, refusing to see anyone except the producer, doing all his business over the telephone—and watching the final result to ensure that his ideas had not been mutilated. The only sign of his connection with the slightly fantastic world of commercial TV was a crate of Crunche in one corner of the workshop. He had sampled one mouthful of this present from the grateful sponsor and had then remembered thankfully that, after all, he was not paid to eat the stuff.

He was working late one Sunday evening, putting the final touches to a new design for a space helmet, when he suddenly realized that he was no longer alone. Slowly he turned from the workbench and faced the door. It had been locked—how could it have been opened so silently? There were two men standing beside it, motionless, watching him. Hans felt his heart trying to climb into his gullet, and summoned up what courage he could to challenge them. At least, he felt thankfully, he had little money here. Then he wondered if, after all, this was a good thing. They might be annoyed. . . .

"Who are you?" he asked. "What are you doing here?"

One of the men moved towards him while the other remained watching alertly from the door. They were both wearing very new overcoats, with hats low down on their heads so that Hans could not see their faces. They were too well dressed, he decided, to be ordinary hold-up men.

"There's no need to be alarmed, Mr. Muller," replied the nearer man, reading his thoughts without difficulty. "This isn't a hold-up. It's official. We're from—Security."

"I don't understand."

The other reached into a portfolio he had been carrying beneath his coat, and pulled out a sheaf of photographs. He riffled through them until he had found the one he wanted.

"You've given us quite a headache, Mr. Muller. It's taken us two weeks to find you—your employers were so secretive. No doubt they were anxious to hide you from their rivals. However, here we are and I'd like you to answer some questions."

"I'm not a spy!" answered Hans indignantly as the meaning of the words penetrated. "You can't do this! I'm a loyal American citizen!"

The other ignored the outburst. He handed over the photograph.

"Do you recognize this?" he said.

"Yes. It's the inside of Captain Zipp's spaceship."

"And you designed it?"

"Yes."

Another photograph came out of the file.

"And what about this?"

"That's the Martian city of Paldar, as seen from the air."

"Your own idea?"

"Certainly," Hans replied, now too indignant to be cautious.

"And *this*?"

"Oh, the proton gun. I was quite proud of that."

"Tell me, Mr Muller—are these all your own ideas?"

"Yes, *I* don't steal from other people."

His questioner turned to his companion and spoke for a few minutes in a voice too low for Hans to hear. They seemed to reach agreement on some point, and the conference was over before Hans could make his intended grab at the telephone.

"I'm sorry," continued the intruder. "But there has been a serious leak. It may be—uh—accidental, even unconscious, but that does not affect the issue. We will have to investigate you. Please come with us."

There was such power and authority in the stranger's voice that Hans began to climb into his overcoat without a murmur. Somehow, he no longer doubted his visitors' credentials and never thought of asking for any proof. He was worried, but not yet seriously alarmed. Of course, it was obvious what had happened. He remembered hearing about a science-fiction writer during the war who had described the atom bomb with disconcerting accuracy. When so much secret research was going on, such accidents were bound to occur. He wondered just what it was he had given away.

At the doorway, he looked back into his workshop and at the men who were following him.

"It's all a ridiculous mistake," he said. "If I *did* show anything secret in the programme, it was just a coincidence. I've never done anything to annoy the FBI."

It was then that the second man spoke at last, in very bad English and with a most peculiar accent.

"What is the FBI?" he asked.

But Hans didn't hear him. He had just seen the spaceship.

Feathered Friend

To the best of my knowledge, there's never been a regulation that forbids one to keep pets in a space station. No one ever thought it was necessary—and even had such a rule existed, I am quite certain that Sven Olsen would have ignored it.

With a name like that, you will picture Sven at once as a six-foot-six Nordic giant, built like a bull and with a voice to match. Had this been so, his chances of getting a job in space would have been very slim; actually he was a wiry little fellow, like most of the early spacers, and managed to qualify easily for the 150-pound bonus that kept so many of us on a reducing diet.

Sven was one of our best construction men, and excelled at the tricky and specialized work of collecting assorted girders as they floated around in free fall, making them do the slow-motion, three-dimensional ballet that would get them into their right positions, and fusing the pieces together when they were precisely dovetailed into the intended pattern. I never tired of watching him and his gang as the station grew under their hands like a giant jigsaw puzzle; it was a skilled and difficult job, for a space suit is not the most convenient of garbs in which to work. However, Sven's team had one great advantage over the construction gangs you see putting up skyscrapers down on Earth. They could step back and admire their handi-work without being abruptly parted from it by gravity. . . .

Don't ask me why Sven wanted a pet, or why he chose the one he did. I'm not a psychologist, but I must admit that his selection was very sensible. Claribel weighed practically nothing, her food requirements were infinitesimal—and she was not worried, as most animals would have been, by the absence of gravity.

I first became aware that Claribel was aboard when I was sitting in the little cubbyhole laughingly called my office, checking through my lists of technical stores to decide what items we'd be running out of next. When I heard the musical whistle beside my ear, I assumed that it had come over the station intercom, and waited for an announcement to follow. It didn't; instead, there was a long and involved pattern of melody that made me look up with such a start that I forgot all about the angle beam just behind my head. When the stars had ceased to explode before my eyes, I had my first view of Claribel.

She was a small yellow canary, hanging in the air as motion-less as a hummingbird—and with much less effort, for her wings were quietly folded along her sides. We stared at each other for a minute; then, before I had quite recovered my wits, she did a curious kind of backward loop I'm sure no earthbound canary had ever managed, and departed with a few leisurely flicks. It was quite obvious that she'd already learned how to operate in the absence of gravity, and did not believe in doing unnecessary work.

Sven didn't confess to her ownership for several days, and by that time it no longer mattered, because Claribel was a general pet. He had smuggled her up on the last ferry from

Earth, when he came back from leave—partly, he claimed, out of sheer scientific curiosity. He wanted to see just how a bird would operate when it had no weight but could still use its wings.

Claribel thrived and grew fat. On the whole, we had little trouble concealing our unauthorized guest when VIP's from Earth came visiting. A space station has more hiding places than you can count; the only problem was that Claribel got rather noisy when she was upset, and we sometimes had to think fast to explain the curious peeps and whistles that came from ventilating shafts and storage bulkheads. There were a couple of narrow escapes—but then who would dream of looking for a canary in a space station?

We were now on twelve-hour watches, which was not as bad as it sounds, since you need little sleep in space. Though of course there is no "day" and "night" when you are floating in permanent sunlight, it was still convenient to stick to the terms. Certainly when I woke up that "morning" it felt like 6 a.m. on Earth. I had a nagging headache, and vague memories of fitful, disturbed dreams. It took me ages to undo my bunk straps, and I was still only half awake when I joined the remainder of the duty crew in the mess. Breakfast was unusually quiet, and there was one seat vacant.

"Where's Sven?" I asked, not very much caring.

"He's looking for Claribel," someone answered. "Says he can't find her anywhere. She usually wakes him up."

Before I could retort that she usually woke me up, too, Sven came in through the doorway, and we could see at once that something was wrong. He slowly opened his hand, and there lay a tiny bundle of yellow feathers, with two clenched claws sticking up pathetically into the air.

"What happened?" we asked, all equally distressed.

"I don't know," said Sven mournfully. "I just found her like this."

"Let's have a look at her," said Jock Duncan, our cook-doctor-dietitian. We all waited in hushed silence while he held Claribel against his ear in an attempt to detect any heartbeat.

Presently he shook his head. "I can't hear anything, but that doesn't prove she's dead. I've never listened to a canary's heart," he added rather apologetically.

"Give her a shot of oxygen," suggested somebody, pointing to the green-banded emergency cylinder in its recess beside the door. Everyone agreed that this was an excellent idea, and Claribel was tucked snugly into a face mask that was large enough to serve as a complete oxygen tent for her.

To our delighted surprise, she revived at once. Beaming broadly, Sven removed the mask, and she hopped on to his finger. She gave her series of "Come to the cook-house, boys" trills—then promptly keeled over again.

"I don't get it," lamented Sven. "What's wrong with her? She's never done this before."

For the last few minutes, something had been tugging at my memory. My mind seemed to be very sluggish that morning, as if I was still unable to cast off the burden of sleep. I felt that I could do with some of that oxygen—but before I could reach the mask, understanding exploded in my brain. I whirled on the duty engineer and said urgently:

"Jim! There's something wrong with the air! That's why Claribel's passed out. I've just remembered that miners used to carry canaries down to warn them of gas."

"Nonsense!" said Jim. "The alarms would have gone off. We've got duplicate circuits, operating independently."

"Er—the second alarm circuit isn't connected up yet," his assistant reminded him. That shook Jim; he left without a word, while we stood arguing and passing the oxygen bottle around like a pipe of peace.

He came back ten minutes later with a sheepish expression. It was one of those accidents that couldn't possibly happen; we'd had one of our rare eclipses by Earth's shadow that night; part of the air purifier had frozen up, and the single alarm in the circuit had failed to go off. Half a million dollars' worth of chemical and electronic engineering had let us down completely. Without Claribel, we should soon have been slightly dead.

So now, if you visit any space station, don't be surprised if you hear an inexplicable snatch of bird song. There's no need to be alarmed: on the contrary, in fact. It will mean that you're doubly safeguarded, at practically no extra expense.

The Sentinel

The next time you see the full Moon high in the south, look carefully at its right-hand edge and let your eye travel upward along the curve of the disk. Round about two o'clock you will notice a small, dark oval: anyone with normal eyesight can find it quite easily. It is the great walled plain, one of the finest on the Moon, known as the Mare Crisium—the Sea of Crises. Three hundred miles in diameter, and almost completely surrounded by a ring of magnificent mountains, it had never been explored until we entered it in the late summer of 1996.

Our expedition was a large one. We had two heavy freighters which had flown our supplies and equipment from the main lunar base in the Mare Serenitatis, five hundred miles away. There were also three small rockets which were intended for short-range transport over regions which our surface vehicles couldn't cross. Luckily, most of the Mare Crisium is very flat. There are none of the great crevasses so common and so dangerous elsewhere, and very few craters or mountains of any size. As far as we could tell, our powerful caterpillar tractors would have no difficulty in taking us wherever we wished to go.

I was geologist—or selenologist, if you want to be pedantic—

in charge of the group exploring the southern region of the Mare. We had crossed a hundred miles of it in a week, skirting the foothills of the mountains along the shore of what was once the ancient sea, some thousand million years before. When life was beginning on Earth, it was already dying here. The waters were retreating down the flanks of those stupendous cliffs, retreating into the empty heart of the Moon. Over the land which we were crossing, the tideless ocean had once been half a mile deep, and now the only trace of moisture was the hoar-frost one could sometimes find in caves which the searing sunlight never penetrated.

We had begun our journey early in the slow lunar dawn, and still had almost a week of Earth time before nightfall. Half a dozen times a day we would leave our vehicle and go outside in the space suits to hunt for interesting minerals, or to place markers for the guidance of future travellers. It was an uneventful routine. There is nothing hazardous or even particularly exciting about lunar exploration. We could live comfortably for a month in our pressurized tractors, and if we ran into trouble we could always radio for help and sit tight until one of the spaceships came to our rescue.

I said just now that there was nothing exciting about lunar exploration, but of course that isn't true. One could never grow tired of those incredible mountains, so much more rugged than the gentle hills of Earth. We never knew, as we rounded the capes and promontories of that vanished sea, what new splendours would be revealed to us. The whole southern curve of the Mare Crisium is a vast delta where a score of rivers once found their way into the ocean, fed perhaps by the torrential rains that must have lashed the mountains in the brief volcanic age when the Moon was young. Each of these ancient valleys was an invitation, challenging us to climb into the unknown uplands beyond. But we had a hundred miles still to cover, and could only look longingly at the heights which others must scale.

We kept Earth time aboard the tractor, and precisely at 2200 hours the final radio message would be sent out to Base and we would close down for the day. Outside, the rocks would still be burning beneath the almost vertical sun, but to us it was night until we awoke again eight hours later. Then one of us would prepare breakfast, there would be a great buzzing of electric razors, and someone would switch on the short-wave radio from Earth. Indeed, when the smell of frying sausages began to fill the cabin, it was sometimes hard to believe that we were not back on our own world—everything was so normal and homely, apart from the feeling of decreased weight and the unnatural slowness with which objects fell.

It was my turn to prepare breakfast in the corner of the main cabin that served as a galley. I can remember that moment quite vividly after all these years, for the radio had just played one of my favourite melodies, the old Welsh air "David of the White Rock." Our driver was already outside in his space suit, inspecting our caterpillar treads. My assistant, Louis Garnett, was up forward in the control position, making some belated entries in yesterday's log.

As I stood by the frying pan waiting, like any terrestrial housewife, for the sausages to brown, I let my gaze wander idly over the mountain walls which covered the whole of the southern horizon, marching out of sight to east and west below the curve of the Moon. They seemed only a mile or two from the tractor, but I knew that the nearest was twenty miles away. On the Moon, of course, there is no loss of detail with distance—none of that almost imperceptible haziness which softens and sometimes transfigures all far-off things on Earth.

Those mountains were ten thousand feet high, and they

climbed steeply out of the plain as if ages ago some subterranean eruption had smashed them skyward through the molten crust. The base of even the nearest was hidden from sight by the steeply curving surface of the plain, for the Moon is a very little world, and from where I was standing the horizon was only two miles away.

I lifted my eyes towards the peaks which no man had ever climbed, the peaks which, before the coming of terrestrial life, had watched the retreating oceans sink sullenly into their graves, taking with them the hope and the morning promise of a world. The sunlight was beating against those ramparts with a glare that hurt the eyes, yet only a little way above them the stars were shining steadily in a sky blacker than a winter midnight on Earth.

I was turning away when my eye caught a metallic glitter high on the ridge of a great promontory thrusting out into the sea thirty miles to the west. It was a dimensionless point of light, as if a star had been clawed from the sky by one of those cruel peaks, and I imagined that some smooth rock surface was catching the sunlight and heliographing it straight into my eyes. Such things were not uncommon. When the Moon is in her second quarter, observers on Earth can sometimes see the great ranges in the Oceanus Procellarum burning with a blue-white iridescence as the sunlight flashes from their slopes and leaps again from world to world. But I was curious to know what kind of rock could be shining so brightly up there, and I climbed into the observation turret and swung our four-inch telescope round to the west.

I could see just enough to tantalize me. Clear and sharp in the field of vision, the mountain peaks seemed only half a mile away, but whatever was catching the sunlight was still too small to be resolved. Yet it seemed to have an elusive symmetry, and the summit upon which it rested was curiously flat. I stared for a long time at that glittering enigma, straining my eyes into space, until presently a smell of burning from the galley told me that our breakfast sausages had made their quarter-million-mile journey in vain.

All that morning we argued our way across the Mare Crisium while the western mountains reared higher in the sky. Even when we were out prospecting in the space suits, the discussion would continue over the radio. It was absolutely certain, my companions argued, that there had never been any form of intelligent life on the Moon. The only living things that had ever existed there were a few primitive plants and their slightly less degenerate ancestors. I knew that as well as anyone, but there are times when a scientist must not be afraid to make a fool of himself.

"Listen," I said at last, "I'm going up there, if only for my own peace of mind. That mountain's less than twelve thousand feet high—that's only two thousand under Earth gravity—and I can make the trip in twenty hours at the outside. I've always wanted to go up into those hills, anyway, and this gives me an excellent excuse."

"If you don't break your neck," said Garnett, "you'll be the laughing-stock of the expedition when we get back to Base. That mountain will probably be called Wilson's Folly from now on."

"I won't break my neck," I said firmly. "Who was the first man to climb Pico and Helicon?"

"But weren't you rather younger in those days?" asked Louis gently.

"That," I said with great dignity, "is as good a reason as any for going."

We went to bed early that night, after driving the tractor to within half a mile of the promontory. Garnett was coming with me in the morning; he was a good climber, and had often been with me on such exploits before. Our driver was only too glad to be left in charge of the machine.

At first sight, those cliffs seemed completely unscalable, but to anyone with a good head for heights, climbing is easy on a world where all weights are only a sixth of their normal value. The real danger in lunar mountaineering lies in overconfidence; a six-hundred-foot drop on the Moon can kill you just as thoroughly as a hundred-foot fall on Earth.

We made our first halt on a wide ledge about four thousand feet above the plain. Climbing had not been very difficult, but my limbs were stiff with the unaccustomed effort, and I was glad of the rest. We could still see the tractor as a tiny metal insect far down at the foot of the cliff, and we reported our progress to the driver before starting on the next ascent.

Inside our suits it was comfortably cool, for the refrigeration units were fighting the fierce sun and carrying away the body heat of our exertions. We seldom spoke to each other, except to pass climbing instructions and to discuss our best plan of ascent. I do not know what Garnett was thinking, probably that this was the craziest goose chase he had ever embarked upon. I more than half agreed with him, but the joy of climbing, the knowledge that no man had ever gone this way before and the exhilaration of the steadily widening landscape gave me all the reward I needed.

I don't think I was particularly excited when I saw in front of us the wall of rock I had first inspected through the telescope from thirty miles away. It would level off about fifty feet above our heads, and there on the plateau would be the thing that had lured me over these barren wastes. It was almost certainly, nothing more than a boulder splintered ages ago by a falling meteor, and with its cleavage planes still fresh and bright in this incorruptible, unchanging silence.

There were no handholds on the rock face, and we had to use a grapnel. My tired arms seemed to gain new strength as I swung the three-pronged metal anchor round my head and sent it sailing up towards the stars. The first time it broke loose and came falling slowly back when we pulled the rope. On the third attempt, the prongs gripped firmly and our combined weights could not shift it.

Garnett looked at me anxiously. I could tell that he wanted to go first, but I smiled back at him through the glass of my helmet and shook my head. Slowly, taking my time, I began the final ascent.

Even with my space suit, I weighed only forty pounds here, so I pulled myself up hand over hand without bothering to use my feet. At the rim I paused and waved to my companion; then I scrambled over the edge and stood upright, staring ahead of me.

You must understand that until this very moment I had been almost completely convinced that there could be nothing strange or unusual for me to find here. Almost, but not quite; it was that haunting doubt that had driven me forward. Well, it was a doubt no longer, but the haunting had scarcely begun.

I was standing on a plateau perhaps a hundred feet across. It had once been smooth—too smooth to be natural—but falling meteors had pitted and scored its surface through immeasurable aeons. It had been levelled to support a glittering, roughly pyramidal structure, twice as high as a man, that was set in rock like a gigantic many-faceted jewel.

Probably no emotion at all filled my mind in those first few seconds. Then I felt a great lifting of my heart, and a strange, inexpressible joy. For I loved the Moon, and now I knew that

the creeping moss of Aristarchus and Eratosthenes was not the
only life she had brought forth in her youth. The old, discredited
dream of the first explorers was true. There had, after all, been a
lunar civilization—and I was the first to find it. That I had come
perhaps a hundred million years too late did not distress me; it
was enough to have come at all.

My mind was beginning to function normally, to analyse and
to ask questions. Was this a building, a shrine—or something
for which my language had no name? If a building, then why
was it erected in so uniquely inaccessible a spot? I wondered if
it might be a temple, and I could picture the adepts of some
strange priesthood calling on their gods to preserve them as the
life of the Moon ebbed with the dying oceans, and calling on
their gods in vain.

I took a dozen steps forward to examine the thing more
closely, but some sense of caution kept me from going too near.
I knew a little of archaeology, and tried to guess the cultural
level of the civilization that must have smoothed this mountain
and raised the glittering mirror surfaces that still dazzled my
eyes.

The Egyptians could have done it, I thought, if their work-
men had possessed whatever strange materials these far more
ancient architects had used. Because of the thing's smallness,
it did not occur to me that I might be looking at the handiwork
of a race more advanced than my own. The idea that the Moon
had possessed intelligence at all was still almost too tremendous
to grasp, and my pride would not let me take the final, humili-
ating plunge.

And then I noticed something that set the scalp crawling at
the back of my neck—something so trivial and so innocent
that many would never have noticed it at all. I have said that
the plateau was scarred by meteors; it was also coated inches

deep with the cosmic dust that is always filtering down upon the surface of any world where there are no winds to disturb it. Yet the dust and the meteor scratches ended quite abruptly in a wide circle enclosing the little pyramid, as though an invisible wall was protecting it from the ravages of time and the slow but ceaseless bombardment from space.

There was someone shouting in my earphones, and I realized that Garnett had been calling me for some time. I walked unsteadily to the edge of the cliff and signalled him to join me, not trusting myself to speak. Then I went back towards that circle in the dust. I picked up a fragment of splintered rock and tossed it gently towards the shining enigma. If the pebble had vanished at that invisible barrier I should not have been surprised, but it seemed to hit a smooth, hemispherical surface and slide gently to the ground.

I knew then that I was looking at nothing that could be matched in the antiquity of my own race. This was not a building, but a machine, protecting itself with forces that had challenged Eternity. Those forces, whatever they might be, were still operating, and perhaps I had already come too close. I thought of all the radiations man had trapped and tamed in the past century. For all I knew, I might be as irrevocably doomed as if I had stepped into the deadly, silent aura of an unshielded atomic pile.

I remember turning then towards Garnett, who had joined me and was now standing motionless at my side. He seemed quite oblivious to me, so I did not disturb him but walked to the edge of the cliff in an effort to marshal my thoughts. There below me lay the Mare Crisium—Sea of Crises, indeed—strange and weird to most men, but reassuringly familiar to me. I lifted my eyes towards the crescent Earth, lying in her cradle of stars, and I wondered what her clouds had covered when these unknown builders had finished their work. Was it the steaming jungle of the Carboniferous, the bleak shoreline over which the first amphibians must crawl to conquer the land—or, earlier still, the long loneliness before the coming of life?

Do not ask me why I did not guess the truth sooner—the truth that seems so obvious now. In the first excitement of my discovery, I had assumed without question that this crystalline apparition had been built by some race belonging to the Moon's remote past, but suddenly, and with overwhelming force, the belief came to me that it was as alien to the Moon as I myself.

In twenty years we had found no trace of life but a few degenerate plants. No lunar civilization, whatever its doom, could have left but a single token of its existence.

I looked at the shining pyramid again, and the more remote it seemed from anything that had to do with the Moon. And suddenly I felt myself shaking with a foolish, hysterical laughter, brought on by excitement and over-exertion: for I had imagined that the little pyramid was speaking to me and was saying: "Sorry, I'm a stranger here myself."

It has taken us twenty years to crack that invisible shield and to reach the machine inside those crystal walls. What we could not understand, we broke at last with the savage might of atomic power and now I have seen the fragments of the lovely, glittering thing I found up there on the mountain.

They are meaningless. The mechanisms—if indeed they are mechanisms—of the pyramid belong to a technology that lies far beyond our horizon, perhaps to the technology of paraphysical forces.

The mystery haunts us all the more now that the other planets have been reached and we know that only Earth has ever been the home of intelligent life in our Universe. Nor could any lost civilization of our own world have built that machine, for the thickness of the meteoric dust on the plateau has enabled us to measure its age. It was set there upon its mountain before life had emerged from the seas of Earth.

When our world was half its present age, *something* from the stars swept through the Solar System, left this token of its passage, and went again upon its way. Until we destroyed it, that machine was still fulfilling the purpose of its builders; and so to that purpose, here is my guess.

Nearly a hundred thousand million stars are turning in the circle of the Milky Way, and long ago other races on the worlds of other suns must have scaled and passed the heights that we have reached. Think of such civilizations, far back in time against the fading afterglow of Creation, masters of a Universe so young that life as yet had come only to a handful of worlds. Theirs would have been a loneliness we cannot imagine, the loneliness of gods looking out across infinity and finding none to share their thoughts.

They must have searched the star clusters as we have searched the planets. Everywhere there would be worlds, but they would be empty or peopled with crawling, mindless things. Such was our own Earth, the smoke of the great volcanoes still staining the skies, when that first ship of the peoples of the dawn came sliding in from the abyss beyond Pluto. It passed the frozen outer worlds, knowing that life could play no part in their destinies. It came to rest among the inner planets, warming themselves around the fire of the Sun and waiting for their stories to begin.

Those wanderers must have looked on Earth, circling safely in the narrow zone between fire and ice, and must have guessed that it was the favourite of the Sun's children. Here, in the distant future, would be intelligence; but there were countless stars before them still, and they might never come this way again.

So they left a sentinel, one of millions they have scattered throughout the Universe, watching over all worlds with the promise of life. It was a beacon that down the ages has been patiently signalling the fact that no one had discovered it.

Perhaps you understand now why that crystal pyramid was set upon the Moon instead of on the Earth. Its builders were not concerned with races still struggling up from savagery. They would be interested in our civilization only if we proved our fitness to survive—by crossing space and so escaping from the Earth, our cradle. That is the challenge that all intelligent races must meet, sooner or later. It is a double challenge, for it depends in turn upon the conquest of atomic energy and the last choice between life and death.

Once we had passed that crisis, it was only a matter of time before we found the pyramid and forced it open. Now its signals have ceased, and those whose duty it is will be turning their minds upon Earth. Perhaps they wish to help our infant civilization. But they must be very, very old, and the old are often insanely jealous of the young.

I can never look now at the Milky Way without wondering from which of those banked clouds of stars the emissaries are coming. If you will pardon so commonplace a simile, we have set off the fire alarm and have nothing to do but to wait.

I do not think we will have to wait for long.

Bibliography: books by *Arthur C. Clarke*

Novels

THE SANDS OF MARS: Sidgwick
and Jackson, 1951
ISLANDS IN THE SKY: Sidgwick
and Jackson, 1952
PRELUDE TO SPACE: Sidgwick and
Jackson, 1953
AGAINST THE FALL OF NIGHT:
New York, Gnome Press, 1953
CHILDHOOD'S END: Sidgwick and
Jackson, 1954
EARTHLIGHT: Muller, 1955
THE CITY AND THE STARS:
Muller, 1956
THE DEEP RANGE: Muller, 1957
ACROSS THE SEA OF STARS
(includes *Childhood's End, Earthlight,*
and eighteen short stories): New
York, Harcourt, 1959
A FALL OF MOONDUST: Gollancz,
1961
FROM THE OCEANS, FROM THE
STARS (includes *The Deep Range, The
City and the Stars,* and twenty-four
short stories): New York, Harcourt,
1962
DOLPHIN ISLAND: A STORY OF
THE PEOPLE OF THE SEA:
Gollancz, 1963
PRELUDE TO MARS (includes
Prelude to Space, The Sands of Mars, and
sixteen short stories): New York,
Harcourt, 1965
2001: A SPACE ODYSSEY:
Hutchinson, 1968
GLIDE PATH: Sidgwick and Jackson,
1969
THE LION OF COMARRE and
AGAINST THE FALL OF
NIGHT: Gollancz, 1970
THE WIND FROM THE SUN:
Gollancz, 1972

RENDEZVOUS WITH RAMA:
Gollancz, 1973
IMPERIAL EARTH: Gollancz, 1975
THE FOUNTAINS OF PARADISE:
Gollancz, 1979
2010: ODYSSEY TWO: Granada,
1982

Short Stories

EXPEDITION TO EARTH (eleven
science fiction stories): Sidgwick and
Jackson, 1954
TALES FROM THE WHITE HART:
New York, Ballantine, 1957
THE OTHER SIDE OF THE SKY:
Gollancz, 1961
REACH FOR TOMORROW:
Gollancz, 1962
TALES OF TEN WORLDS: Gollancz,
1963
THE NINE BILLION NAMES OF
GOD: New York, Harcourt, 1967
OF TIME AND STARS: Gollancz,
1972, 1983

Screenplay

2001: A SPACE ODYSSEY: with
Stanley Kubrick, 1968

Non-fiction

INTERPLANETARY FLIGHT: AN
INTRODUCTION TO
ASTRONAUTICS: Temple, 1950;
revised edition, Temple, 1960
THE EXPLORATION OF SPACE:
Temple, 1951; revised edition, New
York, Harper, 1959
THE YOUNG TRAVELLER IN
SPACE: Phoenix House, 1954
THE EXPLORATION OF THE
MOON: with R. A. Smith, Muller,
1954

Bibliography

THE COAST OF CORAL: Muller, 1956

THE MAKING OF A MOON: THE STORY OF THE EARTH SATELLITE PROGRAMME: Muller, 1957; revised edition, New York, Harper, 1958

THE REEFS OF TAPROBANE: UNDERWATER ADVENTURES AROUND CEYLON: Muller, 1957

VOICE ACROSS THE SEA: Muller, 1958

BOY BENEATH THE SEA: with Mike Wilson, New York, Harper, 1958

THE CHALLENGE OF THE SPACESHIP: PREVIEWS OF TOMORROW'S WORLD: Muller, 1960

THE FIRST FIVE FATHOMS: A GUIDE TO UNDERWATER ADVENTURE: with Mike Wilson, New York, Harper, 1960

THE CHALLENGE OF THE SEA: Muller, 1960

INDIAN OCEAN ADVENTURE: with Mike Wilson, Barker, 1962

PROFILES OF THE FUTURE: AN INQUIRY INTO THE LIMITS OF THE POSSIBLE: Gollancz, 1962

THE TREASURE OF THE GREAT REEF: with Mike Wilson, Barker, 1964

MAN AND SPACE: with the editors of *Life* magazine, New York, Time, 1964

VOICES FROM THE SKY: PREVIEWS OF THE COMING SPACE AGE: Gollancz, 1966

Editor – TIME PROBE: THE SCIENCE IN SCIENCE FICTION: Gollancz, 1967

Editor – THE COMING OF THE SPACE AGE: FAMOUS ACCOUNTS OF MAN'S PROBING OF THE UNIVERSE: Gollancz, 1967

THE PROMISE OF SPACE: Hodder and Stoughton, 1968

FIRST ON THE MOON: WITH THE ASTRONAUTS: Boston, Little Brown, 1970

THE LOST WORLDS OF 2001: New York, New American Library, 1972

BEYOND JUPITER: with Chesley Bonestell, Boston, Little Brown, 1972

INTO SPACE: with Robert Silverberg, New York, Harper, 1972

INDIAN OCEAN TREASURE: with Mike Wilson, Sidgwick and Jackson, 1972

REPORT ON PLANET THREE: Gollancz, 1972

THE VIEW FROM SERENDIP: Gollancz, 1978

ARTHUR C. CLARKE'S MYSTERIOUS WORLD: with Simon Welfare and John Fairley, Collins 1980